Stirring Attraction

Stirring Attraction

A SECOND SHOT NOVEL

SARA JANE STONE

AVONIMPULSE

An Imprint of HarperCollinsPublishers

Excerpt from *Serving Trouble* copyright © 2016 by Sara Jane Stone.
Excerpt from *Change of Heart* copyright © 2016 by Tina Klinesmith.
Excerpt from *Montana Hearts: True Country Hero* copyright © 2016 Darlene Panzera.
Excerpt from *Once and For All* copyright © 2016 by Cheryl Etchison Smith.

EPub Edition JUNE 2016 ISBN: 9780062423863
Print ISBN: 9780062423870

10 9 8 7 6 5 4 3 2 1

*For my grandmothers,
two of the strongest women I have ever had
the pleasure of knowing*

Acknowledgments

I OWE AMANDA Bergeron a huge thank you for allowing me to follow my characters. When I sat down to write Lily and Dominic's story, I had a rough outline in my head. I never wrote it down or shared it with my editor. I allowed the suspense elements to unfold as I wrote without trying to fit the pieces into an overall plan. I focused on what my characters felt in each scene and each moment. And I have never had so much fun writing. Thank you, Amanda!

As always a heartfelt thank you to Jill Marsal for being the best agent ever. I also owe a debt of gratitude to everyone at Avon Impulse—thank you for everything you do, from the covers to the marketing to the publicity!

To my amazing sister and all of her medical school friends, thank you for taking the time to answer all of my questions about gunshot wounds, damaged nerves, and knife wounds. And for the text messages sent five minutes after you respond that politely ask: "This is for a book, right?"

I also must thank my husband for taking the children for days and nights at a time so that I could escape from the house and write. To my awesome kids—JJ and AB—one day I promise to teach you the meaning of the word "deadline." And no, it does not mean "eating cupcakes after sending a book to an editor." Your kindergarten and preschool teachers gave me some funny looks at pickup when you shared that definition with them.

To all of my readers, thank you for embracing the Second Shot series. I hope you're ready for Josh and Caroline's story, *Mixing Temptation*!

Prologue

"YOU PAINTED YOUR toenails pink."

Dominic Fairmore stared at Lily's bumble-gum-colored nails. He didn't trust himself to look up. Downstairs, his dad's dogs made the familiar trip to the water bowl and back, probably stopping to sniff the bag of Chinese takeout he'd abandoned on the kitchen table. The animals' nails tapped against the hardwood floors, but otherwise silence filled the farmhouse. His little sister was at the beach and his dad was pulling a double at Forever, Oregon's woefully understaffed police station. And yeah, he kept track of their locations because at twenty-two he still lived at home.

Lily raised one perfect eyebrow. "I have two hours before my mom expects me home and you're looking at my toenails?"

Her ironic tone pushed him damn close to his breaking point. He'd take her. Here. Now. Against the wall, pictures falling to the floor. Because he knew she reserved her humor for him. The rest of Forever saw a blond-haired, blue-eyed woman who charmed a roomful of five-year-olds day after day. A girl who'd been born here, grown up here, and put herself through the local university while still living at home to care for her wheelchair-bound mother and alcoholic father.

But Dominic saw the only girl he'd ever loved. If he closed his eyes, he could still picture her walking down the halls of their high school. She'd been one year ahead of him. She'd graced the dreary high school halls with her sunshine smile and confidence. And yeah, her short skirts.

He'd memorized the way her cheerleader's outfit teased her thighs while she led the squad her senior year. He'd been a junior, but already shepherding the football team to one victory after another. And sometimes it felt like he busted his ass on the field and won the game just to see her smile . . .

But he couldn't close his eyes and block out the way Lily looked right now. His gaze drifted up her calves. Every inch of bare skin wrapped around his heart like a noose. He took in the curve of her thighs and tried to go slow. His jaw tightened and his eyes disobeyed.

Fuck slow.

His gaze locked on the slip of fabric disappearing between her legs.

"Your panties match your toenails," he growled. There wasn't a hint of humor in his voice. He couldn't picture laughing now. In two days, he'd wreck her heart. He would shatter their love and leave her with nothing but memories and the promise that he'd come back.

I swear I'll come back for her.

But so much could change while he was on the other side of the country training to be all he could be. And later, once he deployed, on the other side of the world.

Two more days. Two more nights. How many times could he make love to this woman before they ran out of time?

"Are you sure they match?" she teased. Her fingers brushed the waistband of her panties and then her thumbs slipped beneath the pink fabric.

His hands formed tight fists at his sides, watching as she drew her underwear down to her toes. Her upper body stole away his view of the blond curls, instead offering the sight of her full, bare breasts hovering in front of her legs. Long locks of blond hair drifted down as she compared the color of her underwear to her nail polish.

"Lily," he growled, and stepped closer.

She glanced up at him slowly, as if she knew every movement of her body turned him on and pushed him closer to that place where he lost control. But hell, after five years together, Lily Greene damn well knew how to drive him crazy with lust and longing.

"My nails are a light pink. I think the bottle said 'Ballet Slipper.' But my underwear is closer to fuchsia." She tossed her panties at him. "See?"

Years of training on the football field kicked in and he caught the slip of fabric in his right hand. "You're right," he said and he took a step forward. He threw her underwear down to the carpet without bothering to study them.

"You need to be home in two hours?" he asked.

Her teasing smile faded at the reminder of the reality beyond the bedroom walls. "You know I do."

"We might not have time for the Chinese food." He momentarily blocked his view as he drew his "Go Army!" T-shirt over his head. He discarded the reminder of where he was heading in two days' time. He wanted to leave this town and the dead-end future it promised, but not Lily.

"I hate Chinese," she said.

She reached forward and grabbed on to the belt buckle his father had given him after he won the state championship with his high school football team. He pressed his palms flat against the wall, one on either side of her head. He couldn't touch her. Not yet.

"I know." He allowed her to pull him close, her fingers working to free his belt and undo his jeans. "I didn't want to run the risk that you would want to eat first."

She smiled as her hands won the battle with his belt. Drawing his zipper down, she leaned forward and whispered in his ear. "Smart man." Her hands pushed his pants over his hips and then went in search of their target.

"Lily," he gasped as her fingers wrapped around the part of his body that thought "slow" spelled disaster. Hell, it just might. He wanted her so damn much he might come in her hand. "Careful," he added. "Or I'll be about as useful as I was the first time. In the front seat of my truck."

"Have as much self-control now as you did at seventeen?" she challenged, her hand moving up and down now.

"You know it." He took his right hand off the wall and cupped her jaw. Angling her lips up to meet his, he kissed her. He knew her mouth. He'd memorized the way she liked his tongue to tease hers.

His hand moved down her neck and over her shoulder. His fingers froze, hovering on her collarbone. He knew the feel of her soft skin as well as he knew his own. But dammit, he couldn't take the weight of her breast in his hand, her nipple brushing against his palm, and still maintain control.

She broke the kiss. "Don't hold back, Dominic," she whispered. "You never have before. Don't start now. You know how to touch me. You're the only one—"

His growl cut off her hushed words. He was the only one who knew the color of her panties. The only man in her bed. The only one who heard her sly humor. And yeah, the only man in Forever, Oregon, who loved her.

For now . . .

Possession unleashed his need and he cupped her breast. He felt the weight against his hand as his thumb drew small circles around her nipple.

Damn right, he knew how to touch her. His other hand abandoned the wall and reached for her hips. He gripped her, holding tight, pinning her against the wall.

"Release me, Lily," he demanded, his forehead touching hers. "Now."

She obeyed, and her hands moved to his bare back.

Holding tight to his shoulders, she raised her right leg and wrapped it around his hips. "Here?" she asked.

He let go of her hip and slipped his hand between her legs. His fingers brushed over her center. *So damn wet.* He slipped his index finger inside. Her hips rocked forward, eager for his touch.

"Here," he confirmed as he drew his fingers away. His other hand let go of her breast and he palmed her bottom. He guided her left leg up until her limbs wrapped around his waist.

"I've got you," he reassured her.

"No, honey," she said, her voice low and rough. "I've got *you.*" She squeezed her thighs as her nails briefly dug into his shoulders.

That voice . . . Those words . . . The woman he'd loved for five long years tore past his restraint.

"Now," she added, rocking her hips forward. "Let's see what these walls are made of."

He slipped inside her. No condom. No barrier between them since she'd started taking the pill. He didn't need to guide himself. He knew how to find home. And Lily was his.

For two more days. . .

He withdrew an inch, then another, and thrust forward. Hard.

"Oh, Dominic," she gasped.

He repeated the motion, loving the sound of his name in that deep voice she reserved for him. Because right now, she was his, dammit.

Maybe one day she'll be mine forever. When I come back and claim her...

He buried himself deep inside her, over and over. The wall shook. But he didn't let up. Harder. Faster. He let his need, his desperation, and yeah, his love for this woman, eclipse everything.

He felt her tighten around him. "Get there, Lily. I know you're close."

"Yes," she called. "Oh ... my ... so, so, so ..."

He recognized the familiar countdown and tightened his grip on her ass, drawing the cheeks apart, offering pressure that he knew would drive her over the edge. Every one of his fingers pressed into her skin.

"Now!" she cried out. "Now, now, now ..."

She slammed her head back against the wall as her back arched. Her fingernails tore at his skin. But the pain didn't distract. He was too close. One more thrust, the wall trembling at her back, and ...

"Aw, fuck," he gasped. "Lily. My Lily." His lips found hers as he came. He welcomed the rush, the pleasure, the relief ... and he hated it.

How many times can I make love to her before I leave? One less now.

She pulled away from the kiss and released her hold on his shoulders. Slowly, she lowered one foot to the ground and then the other. And he let her go, closing his eyes as he stepped back.

"We knocked a picture off the wall," she said with a laugh.

He opened his eyes and glanced at the fallen frame lying facedown on the carpet. "I'll fix it later."

"But right now you have a hankering for an egg roll?" she asked, her tone light.

He looked at the face he knew by heart. Her blond eyebrows formed a pair of perfect arches. She'd probably spent a half hour, maybe more, in front of the mirror, plucking out the stray hairs. He'd watched her do it once, while lying on his bed. His gaze dropped to her lips, curved into a forced smile.

"No, Lily, I don't want an egg roll." He stepped forward and wrapped his arms around her. His naked body pressed against hers. She was tall for a woman. But compared to a man who'd played center for his high school football team? Her cheek pressed against his chest as her arms wrapped around his middle. "I want you," he added gruffly.

Two days and two nights—it would never be enough.

He felt her teardrops running over the hair on his chest. And he waited for the words—*then stay*. She'd let them slip once and then quickly asked to take them back.

"Go ahead and cry, Lil," he murmured, feeling damn near close to tears himself. "I'd take you with me if I could. Hell, I'd marry you tomorrow."

"I know," she said through a sob. The tears were like a river now, flowing down to his abdomen. "I know."

Still, words didn't change the fact that she couldn't leave this town. Her roots were here. So were his. But he was tearing his up. And while his widower father leaned on him for help around the old farmhouse and counted on him to keep his wild little sister from messing up her life, it was nothing compared to Lily's mother. Her mom had spent the past decade struggling with her multiple-sclerosis diagnosis. And Lily had stood by her side every step of the way. She'd attended the local university and gotten her teaching certificate online so that she could care for her mom.

Dominic could silently curse the fact that the girl he loved was saddled with a mom who was losing the ability to care for herself more and more each day. And a dad who drank away his sorrows, rendering himself useless to the woman he'd married and to his daughter. But that wouldn't change a damn thing. Lily's life was here and he was moving across the country for basic training. And after that? The army could send him anywhere in the world.

"Maybe after you serve for a few years, maybe when you come back—"

"I'm coming back for you, Lily. When you're ready, and if you still want me, I'll come back," he said. "But not to stay here, in Forever. You know that, right?"

He waited for her answer. He refused to leave her here, in small-town Oregon, hoping and praying for a future that would never materialize.

"I know," she said.

"I'm not doing this for the money. Hell, the police force paid well. But I can do more."

Be All You Can Be—the slogan resonated with him. He'd known since high school that with the right training he could be one of the best. He could fight on the front lines. And if he had his way, if he succeeded with the option the army had given him under his contract, he'd become an army ranger. Hell, he would have tried for the SEALs, but he wanted to be an infantryman first, focusing on ground combat, not a sailor.

"I love you, Lily," he said. "I'd wait to join up, but now that Josie's heading to college and I don't need to look out for her . . ."

He'd been waiting for this chance since they graduated from high school. He'd stayed to help his dad manage his wild little sister. And he'd tried to make peace with doling out speeding tickets and breaking up parties peopled with underage kids at the town's university. But he couldn't escape the fact that his own mom had died young and suddenly. He wanted to reach for his goals now. He couldn't wait until life turned on him and took him out before he'd gone into the world and proved that he could do so much more.

"I just wish things were different." She drew back and looked up at him. "And I didn't love you quite so much."

A jolt of electricity ran through him as if he'd touch a live wire. He felt like a bastard, but he wanted her love. He wanted everything she had to give.

"I want to serve, Lil. But I've never not wanted you," he said firmly. "How much time do we have left?"

She rose up on tiptoes and glanced over his shoulder at the clock on his wall. "One hour."

"Lie on the bed," he ordered, breaking away from her teary-eyed embrace. "And spread your legs. I'm going to show you how much I love you, Lily."

"You ALL LOOK like you're at a funeral." Lily pushed off the tailgate and headed for the broad-shouldered warriors marching across the yard. She'd spotted Dominic by the barn, flanked by his two best friends, Noah and Ryan. And for a moment she'd hated Dominic's best friends for stealing him away on their last night together. But the feeling faded as they moved closer, their expressions grim, grim, and grimmer.

Tomorrow, Dominic would head to the army, while Noah joined the marines, and Ryan left his family's mansion for the air force. All three of them were leaving, but only Dominic looked like he'd been born to serve. Or maybe that was her eyes playing tricks on her again. She'd always believed that he was bigger, bolder, and better than every other man.

The police force would never be enough for Dominic. He'd joined for his father, his sister, and probably for her. A job that would keep him in Forever, watching over Josie and close to her . . .

"I know." Dominic wrapped his arms around her and drew her close.

"It's my fault, Lily," Noah muttered, kicking the ground.

She looked at Dominic's best friend and saw the blood running down Noah's face, his lip cut. In the firelight, his face looked as if he'd taken a hit. She glanced at Ryan. He'd missed a buttonhole on his shirt. It hung at an odd angle. Had they been fighting? On their last night together?

"What happened?"

"Nothing you need to worry about," Dominic said, releasing his hold on her as he fished his keys out from his pocket. "Let's get you home. I don't want your mom to worry."

Too late. Her mother had worried from Lily's first date with Dominic, wondering—often out loud—if her little girl would hold tight to her parents' belief that she should wait until marriage. And yesterday, in Dominic's bedroom, proved her mother had every reason to be concerned.

"I'm sorry," Noah said. "I shouldn't have—"

"My sister is a big girl, old enough to make her own choices," Dominic cut in.

Noah and Josie?

Lily blinked. She never would have suspected. The town golden boy and Dominic's wild little sister . . . Wow. No wonder Dominic had punched his friend.

She glanced back at Ryan. That still didn't explain the third musketeer's disheveled appearance. What had he been up to on his last night before they went their separate ways, determined to pursue careers that might never bring them back . . . ?

"Let's go, Dom," she murmured, pulling on his hand. Whatever had happened to Ryan, to Noah—she didn't care right now. The minutes were slipping away. And she refused to waste them at a party that felt more like a funeral.

Dominic nodded and led her around to the passenger side of his pickup. He pulled open the door and held it for her as she climbed inside. She rolled down her window while he walked around the rear and hugged his friends, slapping them both on the back in turn. Then she called out her goodbyes. It was like pulling off a Band-Aid. She said the words quickly and turned to stare out into the dark night. She could let Noah and Ryan, the men who'd become her friends through Dominic, go with one swift tearing motion. But the man putting the truck in gear?

She didn't want to let him leave, but she knew as well as he did that a future together was impossible right now. Maybe one day . . .

They drove in silence down the dark country roads, heading for her parents' modest two-bedroom house on the outskirts of town. They sped past the university and Forever's park. When they reached her quiet dead-end street, Dominic pulled over and cut the engine three doors down from her house.

"You'll call me when you get there?" she asked, turning to him as she released her seat belt. "Or as soon as you can?"

He hesitated.

"Please," she added.

"I'll call." He stared into her eyes, his gaze drifting to her mouth and then back up.

She nodded. There was so much more she wanted to say.

I'm happy for you.

Stay safe.

I hate you for leaving.

But she refused to send him off feeling guilty for following his dreams. One day he would come back. Or she'd join him.

She bit her lip. The circumstances surrounding those possibilities—her mother succumbing to MS, or Dominic facing a career-ending injury—she didn't want to hope for those things.

"Lily," he murmured and she met his gaze. "I don't know how to kiss you to make it last—"

"Until the end of basic training? Because after that, I'll find a way to visit you. I can find help for my mom, hire a nurse for a few days. Save up some money and fly down." She spoke fast, the plan taking hold in her mind.

"And after that?" he asked. "I signed on to become a ranger if they'll take me. And there are no guarantees I'll be stationed on the West Coast."

"We can make this work," she insisted. "I'll kiss you goodbye. But it's not forever."

He nodded, but she could see the doubt in his green eyes, and the stark acknowledgment that they might not have a future cut into her. But she pushed aside the pain. They could find a way.

"I'll come back for you," he confirmed. "And when I do, I'll be more. I'm going to give you a future you can count on."

I love you the way you are. I believe in you.

But she couldn't tell him that now. He needed to do this for himself. Joining the army, becoming an elite special soldier, or whatever they called the rangers—that was for him.

"OK," she said.

"And I'll take care of you, Lil. After everything you've

done for your mom, your dad—I'm going to come back for you and—"

"Sweep me off my feet?"

"Yes."

She reached out and touched his cheek. Her hand ran down his throat to his shoulder. She pressed her palm against the hard contours of his pecs, wishing to feel every inch of him.

How do you memorize a man's muscles?

Her gaze drifted back to his lips and she leaned forward. She kept her eyes open until the last second, then she pressed her mouth to his. Her lips parted and she let him in. His tongue touched hers and he kissed her as if he wanted so much more . . .

But they couldn't go any further. Not here. Not now.

"That will have to hold you over for a while," she said, breaking away, her breath coming in sharp gasps. She reached behind her and felt around for the car door handle. "Finish basic training, and I promise I'll kiss you again."

"Lily," he growled.

But she moved too fast, slipping out the passenger side door. She slammed it closed behind her, shutting out his words. And then she ran up the sidewalk, rushing toward the house that held her responsibilities—the people who needed her here, in Forever. Away from the man she loved, the man who was leaving, who didn't need her at his side to survive the day.

The man she wanted in life more than her next breath.

She paused on the front porch steps. Her hand rested on the banister covered in peeling white paint. And she stole one last glance at the truck still parked on the side of the quiet street.

Go. Fight. Be all you can be. And then, come back for me.

Chapter One
_____

Six Years Later. . .

IF IT WASN'T *for Taylor Swift and chocolate brownies, I would be at home wearing size six jeans and enjoying the first Monday of summer break.*

Instead, the potent combination drove Lily to add an extra mile to her morning run. She turned up the volume on Swift's not-so-country album and jogged down Forever's familiar Main Street, trying to shake off the extra calories clinging to her thighs. If she kept going for another ten, maybe fifteen minutes, she'd end up in the park beyond the university. The well-maintained paths weaving through a manicured forest might distract from the fact that she hated running.

But I ate three large brownies at the end-of-year celebration yesterday.

Because who could say no to a six-year-old student with a plate of homemade double-fudge brownies? She might have followed her heart when she'd applied to teach kindergarten in her hometown when she graduated from college. But now, at the ripe old age of twenty-nine, this career was hell on her thighs and waistline.

Not that the kids shouldered all the blame. She'd turned to chocolate for comfort so many times over the past few years that she'd started to wonder if she should follow her father into rehab.

But it hadn't worked for him. He'd been arrested for driving under the influence. And this time the court had ordered him to rehab again. Not that he'd bothered to tell her. She'd received a call from his girlfriend of the moment with the news.

No, she doubted a twelve-step program to abandon chocolate would work for her. Plus, there were some times when she loved her curves. On those days, she welcomed the sugar rush, always promising to run the next day.

And other times . . . well, after struggling to care for her mother toward the end, the handful of reunions with Dominic, followed by the breakups—she'd kissed him goodbye more times than she wanted to count—hadn't she earned a treat? She'd rather have Dominic . . .

But he hadn't returned to Forever. And she'd buried her hope that he ever would after he took two bullets to the chest and one through his hand. He'd almost died in a war-torn country, then again in Germany while on the operating table. But it was the shot that had ripped apart his right hand that might bury him alive. He couldn't go back to the army. The rangers had kicked him out of the only group he'd ever wanted to join.

And he still hadn't come home.

Not to her.

He'd taken a break from his outpatient rehab to meet his niece after she was born. But he'd only stayed for a few days. Lily had been so caught up in school that she hadn't realized he was in town until he'd left again.

The traffic light turned green and she ran across the street, heading for the quiet park. The university students had mostly left for summer vacation. Plus, it was after nine in the morning on a Monday. Most of Forever's locals were at work. She ran past a mother pushing a stroller toward the park's swing set. In the distance, she could see another jogger.

Alone with Taylor Swift. . .

She picked up the pace, determined to push the extra calories clinging to her legs into exile. She had a date tonight with a man who wanted the same things out of life. Marriage. Children. A fellow teacher who wished to settle in Forever, not run away. Ted was the definition of "good man" even if he never tried to back her up against the wall and take her . . .

Stop comparing him to Dominic. Stop waiting for someone who has made it clear he is not coming back.

The playground disappeared from view. She followed the path through the trees. Glimpses of the university's buildings were visible through the bright green leaves, but nothing more. Rounding the bend, she saw a flash of red.

A man. Tall. Broad. Wearing a sweatshirt in June. Who did that? It was hot today even for a summer day.

He drew closer. Running toward her as if he knew her and wanted to say hello. He was moving fast. He was wearing a ski mask. In June . . .

And then he was on top of her.

She hit the pavement and fell back. He came with her. And oh God, he was hitting her. Over and over. She heard screams and hoped the sounds came from someone who would help her. A hit to the jaw. A punch to the gut, this one stinging. And then . . .

Silence.

She'd been the one screaming, her voice high-pitched and terrified. She'd been the one begging for help until the reality sank in. She was alone. In the trees. Out of sight.

"Please . . . stop," she whimpered, struggling to break free. But she wasn't strong enough.

"You ruined everything," a deep voice growled.

She kept her arms over her head, protecting her face. But through the gap she saw dark brown eyes peering at her through the mask.

His pupils are huge. He sounds . . . familiar.

And he looks crazy.

Of course he was. Sane people didn't attack strangers in the park. But who was he?

He hit her forearm and she closed her eyes. The pain distracted from trying to place him. Her arms stung as if she'd been covered in paper cuts. It didn't matter who he was, she just needed him to stop hitting her, stop hurting her . . .

The weight lifted, but the pain remained. She reached for her side. It was wet from his punches.

No, that's not right.

She lifted her palm and saw the blood. And she screamed, over and over, never stopping to breathe. Panic rushed in and held her captive. Her world was reduced to one word.

Help.

No one came. Fear took over, shifting her cries. Screw help. She didn't need a white knight. She needed power, strength, and someone who gave a damn about her.

Dominic.

She called his name. Her voice bordered on hoarse. She inhaled and tried again, staring up at the trees. The branches shifted in the light breeze as if mocking her. Sunbeams slipped through the leaves.

He's not coming.

Her ranger wouldn't rush to her rescue . . .

But he wasn't an army ranger anymore. He'd been injured, rehabbed, and released. And he still hadn't come back to her.

So she'd moved on.

She shouldn't be calling for Dominic. Her new boyfriend—the man who promised a future filled with gentle kisses, romantic adventures, and children. If she made it out of this park . . .

Ted.

She called his name to the trees. The leaves shook, spilling pockets of sunlight on the path. Ted specialized in teaching elementary school kids to read. He was a good man, a kind person . . .

Her vision blurred and the leaves above her merged together. She needed help *now*. She rolled to her side and the pain shifted, but it didn't increase. More wasn't an option. She'd reached her threshold. There was agony and passing out. Those were her only choices

But before she tried to escape the pain, she needed to crawl into the open. She had to save herself. Dominic, Ted, the woman in the park—they weren't rushing to her rescue. She needed to pull herself into the open.

Slowly, she maneuvered onto her belly and raised her left arm. If she could crawl . . .

Dragging her bruised, battered, and possibly sliced forearm over the paved path, she pressed down and pulled her body forward. Her legs scrambled for purchase, but she couldn't find her way onto all fours.

Time distorted like it did when she visited the dentist, and the receptionist insisted on redefining the word "brief." But she made progress. Two slides forward, she saw something pink lying on the path. Her cell phone. She crawled closed and picked it up. Music still blast from the headphones. She turned it over and—

No service.

"Stupid woods," she muttered. "Stupid park."

Still clutching the phone, she started dragging herself forward again. She reached the edge of the path and spotted her saviors. Two girls raced forward as if they'd eaten an entire pan of brownies last night. Or maybe they'd simply spotted her.

Help.

But the cry died before she could part her lips. Her vision blurred. And then—

Nothing.

Chapter Two

"YOU HAVE FIVE minutes to get off your ass and find your pants. Don't bother shaving. We don't have time."

Dominic turned his back on the only appliance in the kitchen he gave a damn about—the coffeemaker—and faced the friend who'd saved his high school football team a time or two with a well-placed field goal. But most of the time, Ryan had missed the uprights. And right now, the town rich kid turned air force officer had kicked one helluva foul.

"How did you get in here?" Dominic asked.

"Your super gave me the key," Ryan said. His dress uniform sparkled under Dominic's crappy overhead lights. Between the severe look on his movie-star face and the medals lining his chest, yeah, Dominic could see how the timid super had handed over the key. Hell, even Dominic was tempted to give in and pull a pair of jeans over his boxer briefs. Maybe find a clean shirt.

"Get dressed," Ryan barked again.

"And if I refuse?" Dominic held tight to his steaming mug with his left hand. He'd given up on sleeping through the lingering pain months ago. Now, he sipped his cup of joe and tried not to think about the future.

"Three minutes now." Ryan glanced down at his watch. "If it takes longer to find your pants and your wallet, I'm heading for an unauthorized absence."

"You're a long way from base. I don't see how three minutes would make a difference—"

"I need you to put down the coffee and put on your pants. They won't let you on the plane in your underwear. And if we miss this flight to Oregon, I won't make it back before my leave is up."

Oregon. Ah hell.

"I'm not getting on a fucking plane. I don't give a damn who sent you to try and bring me home. I'm not going. You're risking your career for a lost cause."

Ryan turned and marched the shiny-ass shoes that matched his sparkly uniform across the apartment. Then he disappeared into the bedroom, leaving Dominic staring into the now empty living area. The space looked as if he'd hired one of the guys who'd served alongside him to play decorator. The worn brown leather couch pointed to a big-ass TV mounted on the wall. A cardboard box sat in front of it.

When Dominic had first moved into the place, a ranger who lived down the road had stopped by for a beer. His buddy had turned over the box and declared it a coffee table. And now, months after leaving the only place where he had ever felt like he belonged—the freaking army—Dominic ate every meal with his feet on that box.

But the sorry state of his rental didn't leave him pining for his dad's farmhouse in Forever, Oregon.

His left hand tightened on his mug to keep his right from dropping the coffee cup to the linoleum. Sure, his brain had fired off the message—hold on to the fucking coffee—but the nerves in his right hand rarely listened anymore.

And neither did Ryan. He could hear his childhood friend opening drawers in his bedroom.

"Hey, careful with my dresser," Dominic called. "I picked that up secondhand. The first owner didn't exactly treat it right."

His friend from what felt like another lifetime—those years before he'd joined the military—ignored him and continued abusing his furniture. Ryan returned a minute later with a pair of faded jeans and plain red T-shirt. "Put down the coffee," he ordered.

Ryan tossed the clothes across the room. But Dominic didn't move to catch them. He'd spent the past few months learning his limitations. Thanks to a trigger-happy terrorist, Dominic's right hand struggled to pick things up. And yeah, there was a laundry list of other things he couldn't do as a result of one bullet through the palm of his hand. Sure, the shots that had nicked his pulmonary artery had nearly cost him his life, but the bullet in his hand had changed his future. He wasn't a soldier anymore. Hell, he wasn't much use to anyone and he damn well knew it.

"If Noah sent you. Or my dad—"

"No one sent me." Ryan's mouth formed a thin line. Either the air force had knocked the playboy humor out of his childhood friend or . . .

Someone had died.

"I wanted to tell you on the plane," Ryan said. "I came to drag your sorry ass back to Oregon because Lily—"

Crash!

His good hand had taken a cue from his right and released the mug. Dominic struggled to stay upright.

"Not Lily," he growled. *"Not Lily."*

Hell, she was the reason he stayed the hell away from Forever. She'd come to visit him in the hospital once he'd been transferred from Germany to a stateside facility. One look into those beautiful blue eyes and dammit, he knew why she'd come. Then she'd spelled it out for him.

Come home. Let me take care of you. This is our fresh start. The one we always talked about. We can get married and—

"I have your attention now?" Ryan said. "Is that the magic word that will get you into your pants? Say her name?"

"What makes you think I still give a damn?" Dominic snapped. "We broke up months ago. For good this time."

Ryan laughed, but the sound was brittle and harsh, devoid of genuine humor. Then he cocked his head and, staring at Dominic, said: "How many women have you slept with since Lily?"

"Fuck you," he fired back. "I haven't spent the past year pining for a woman I can't have. That's your story. Not mine."

"How many?" Ryan challenged again.

None.

He'd come close, messing around with a woman whose name he couldn't recall the next day. But he hadn't slept with her.

Because I didn't give a damn about her.

Because she wasn't Lily.

"You still care about her," Ryan said firmly.

"Yeah," he admitted. What was the point in denying it now? He'd missed his chance. Not that he had one at this point. "But she wanted a family. Marriage, kids. I sent her away."

Because I knew I wasn't good enough for her. Too broken. Too battered.

Dominic looked up at his friend. "And now—"

"She needs you," Ryan said flatly.

"She's not dead." Dominic closed his eyes and let the relief wash over him. It pumped through his veins, one wild rush, and then . . . shit, he felt as if he might faint, right here in his kitchen.

"No, man." Ryan shook his head. "I would have started with the bad news if she'd been killed. And I wouldn't have waited five weeks to come get you."

Five weeks?

He opened his eyes. Had his phone been ringing over

and over, the caller ID flashing familiar Oregon numbers he didn't feel like answering, for over a month?

Probably.

"What happened?" Dominic demanded.

"Someone attacked her."

The muscles in his messed-up hand spasmed. He wanted to hurt whoever did this. Hunt them down and tear into the bastard who'd dared to touch his Lily.

She's not mine. Not anymore.

But dammit, there was one organ beating in his chest that hadn't gotten the message. He would never stop warring with the selfish part of his broken heart that begged him to go home and claim Lily, even though he knew she was better off without him.

"A stranger, possibly drugged or, hell, not taking the drugs prescribed to him," Ryan continued. He spoke quickly as if reciting a report to his commanding officer. "He came at her with a knife while she was jogging."

He let out a noise that sounded a helluva lot like an animal that had been hit. But this bullet, this list of facts, wasn't a kill shot.

"A fucking knife," Dominic growled. "He attacked her with a goddamn knife."

Ryan nodded. "Your sister tried to call you and fill you in."

"I don't answer the phone," he said as he sank to the floor beside the pile of clothes. Coffee and shards of his ceramic mug covered the T-shirt and jeans. He didn't give a damn if the broken pieces cut into him and drew blood.

"Lily's out of the hospital and recovering fine." Ryan claimed a spot on the floor beside him. "Except she's convinced that the cops, including your dad, have it all wrong. Lily believes she was targeted. According to your sister, the physical wounds are healing, but Lily's terrified. Hell, Noah gave her a job bartending at Big Buck's just to get her out of the house. But it has become clear to them that she's not sleeping. She's obsessed with finding out who hurt her."

"And they think I can help her?" Dominic asked, his gaze fixed on the mostly empty living space. He holed up in here twenty-four/seven most days, his feet resting on a damn box. He went to the gym and bought supplies. Nothing more. He'd even given up on the PT for his hand. It wouldn't make a difference. He'd already lost his place with the rangers. He'd lost his dream of providing that best damn future for Lily. He was freaking useless.

"Josie and Noah think that you can make her feel safe. She has driven almost everyone else out of her life," Ryan said.

"Yeah, I'm on that list too. Only I shoved her out months ago. I don't think she'll welcome me back."

"You're a ranger—"

"Was," Dominic cut in. He wasn't fit to help Lily now. And yeah, that fact hurt more than the bullets through his chest.

"I think she'd feel a lot safer with you watching her back than relying on your dad and his deputies. Your father's a good police chief, but he can't have cops patrolling Lily's street all night."

Dominic nodded. Before he'd enlisted, he'd been a cop in Forever. And he knew the department wouldn't protect a woman twenty-four/seven from a criminal they didn't believe had the first clue about where Lily lived.

The air force officer, the only one of the three of them still serving, pushed off the ground and adjusted his uniform. "So are you going to get off your ass, put on some pants, and get on that plane? Or do I need to tell my commanding officer that I won't be there Monday morning because I need to go hunt down a navy SEAL to watch over my best friend's ex because he was too chicken to do it himself?"

"I'll go." Dominic reached for the jeans, shook off the pieces of broken mug, and started pulling them on. "Lily doesn't need a SEAL."

And I'd bet the use of my left hand that she doesn't want me.

But he'd go. He'd look out for the woman he'd loved in what felt like another lifetime. Before a bullet had busted his hand . . . Before he'd lost his place with the rangers . . .

Once he knew that she'd found a way through her fears, he'd disappear again. He didn't have a clue what the future held for him, but he refused to screw with hers.

And hell, while he was home maybe he'd find the scumbag who'd taken a knife to his beautiful, perfect Lily.

Chapter Three

LILY TURNED THE lock and flipped the sign indicating
that the cows were home and Big Buck's Bar was closed
for the night. Through the bar's front window, she saw
a few college-age patrons lingering in the parking lot
and waiting for a cab. She'd personally placed the calls
to Forever's lone taxi service ten minutes before closing.
She might be serving drinks to keep busy until school
started again—and to keep her mind off the attack—but
she couldn't escape her instinct to look after students,
whether they were five or twenty-five.

"Would you like to have a drink before heading
home?"

She glanced over her shoulder. The damaged skin on
her neck pulled taut. Her wounds had scabbed over and
healed. Mostly. The place where he'd slashed her neck had
run deeper than the cuts to her forearms. And the wound
on her side looked as if he'd tried to cut open her stomach

and missed. The doctors had promised a quick recovery, going so far as to smile at the fact that "the crazy random stranger" had stopped short of doing permanent damage.

Lucky me.

But standing in the closed bar, she didn't feel lucky or healed.

"Sure," she said to the dishwasher. Drinking with the reclusive Caroline sounded better than walking through the empty house she'd lived in her entire life. If she went home now, she would spend the rest of the night checking the locks and peering behind doors.

"Good. Wait here. I'll be right back." Caroline offered a curt nod then headed for the swinging door that led to the back room. The Employees Only space housed the bar's office, spare liquor, the kegs, and the dishwasher.

Why did Noah's friend always sound like she was giving out orders? Lily wondered as she headed to the bar. She'd asked Josie and Noah about the quiet, petite woman who avoided the bar's front room whenever there were customers present. But Big Buck's owner and Dominic's little sister, who had somehow found their way to love and a baby after Noah returned from the army, hadn't revealed a word about Caroline.

Lily filled a clean pint glass with water and turned to the whiskey. She heard the door to her left swing open. "What would you like to drink?" she called to the other woman.

"What goes with marionberry pie?" Caroline asked.

Lily glanced over her shoulder and spotted Caroline holding what looked like a homemade pie with a lattice-top crust. Caroline moved surprisingly fast, barely making a sound as she crossed the bar's wooden floorboards, despite wearing what looked like black steel-toed boots.

Who wears combat boots to wash dishes?

But Lily forced the question aside and focused on the bottles lined up against the back of the bar. "I think an Oregon pinot noir would be best. Unless you would prefer whiskey."

"I'll have a glass of the wine." Caroline set the pie dish on the bar's polished wood surface. Then she reached into the pocket of her black cargo shorts and withdrew two forks. "Do you mind eating out of the dish? I didn't want to search for plates."

"Or wash them later?" Lily said with a smile as she uncorked the wine and poured two glasses. She set them by the pie and headed for the service entrance to the bar. Lifting the piece of wood that kept the customers on their side of the space, she slipped out and headed for the stool beside Caroline.

Her coworker nodded, her long dark hair falling over her shoulders.

"You know," Lily said, adjusting her stool so that she could still see the locked front entrance, "I've only been here a week, but that's the second pie Josh Summers has dropped off for you."

"We're friends," Caroline said in a tone that suggested she still didn't quite believe it herself. "And he likes to bake."

"Friends with benefits? I grew up here, surrounded by

loggers. I don't know many who spend their spare time testing new pie recipes," Lily teased, sinking into the moment. When was the last time she'd sat down with someone and gossiped over a glass of wine? Ever since the attack, her friends and coworkers approached every conversation as if they needed to make it crystal clear they had all the sympathy in the world for her.

But she didn't want their pity. And she flat out hated it when they treated her like a child who simply didn't understand when she dared to bring up finding her assailant before he attacked her again.

"Just pie," Caroline said. "I'm not ready for more. When and if I want to date, to have a relationship again, to fall in love, I doubt I'll still be here."

"Planning to move back home?" Lily asked, raising her glass to her lips.

"Or just move on. I can't stay here forever."

"Josh might follow you. I don't know him well, seeing as he went to school in Independence Falls. But we have some mutual friends. I've never seen him smitten or in a long-term relationship. It's been a while since he started baking for you, hasn't it?"

Caroline nodded. "I first ran into Josh over a year ago. He'll probably come to his senses soon and move on. He'll start baking for someone else. So I should enjoy mine while I can."

Caroline reached into the dish and withdrew a forkful of berries covered in crust. But before she raised the utensil to her lips, she glanced at the door.

Lily understood the instinct to search for threats, to

anticipate, and to wait for the attack. It had only been five weeks, but she couldn't remember what it felt like to walk through the day without fear hovering close behind.

"Something happened to you," Lily said, no longer teasing.

"Yes." Then Caroline ate the piece of pie, chewing slowly before returning her fork to the dish. "I think that's why Noah and Josie asked you to cover for April while she's on vacation. They thought I might be able to help you. I know what it's like to feel hunted. To be convinced someone is after you." Caroline glanced up and met her gaze. "And to be wrong."

"I'm not—"

"I'm not saying you are," Caroline cut in. "Maybe the attack was intentional. Maybe the police are wrong."

"They are." Lily picked up her glass and swirled the red liquid.

"It doesn't change the fact that you look at the door, waiting for someone to burst in—"

The unmistakable sound of a key in the lock silenced the conversation. Lily froze, her eyes focused on the door. It had to be Noah, didn't it? He was coming to check on the bar. Or maybe it was Josie. But why would they leave the baby in the middle of the night?

Her grip tightened on her wine glass, preparing to hurl it across the room at the man who might have stolen a key, waiting for his chance to find her and hurt her . . .

The door swung open and a large figure filled the doorway. The light from the parking lot made it difficult to identify his features. But she knew him. She'd know him anywhere.

"Now?" she cried as fury rose up partly driven by the pinot noir. But after all this time, how could Dominic Fairmore walk in holding a freaking key in the middle of the night?

Beside her, the dishwasher moved as if Lily's one-word cry had been a directive. Out of the corner of her eye, she saw Caroline reach for the pie dish. And then it was hurling through the empty bar. The pie collided with the target, covering Lily's ex with a mixture of berries, sugar, and homemade crust. The tin dish dropped to the floor.

"What the hell?" the man roared, whipping the pie from his face.

A year ago, Lily would have laughed at the sight of Dominic covered in dessert. She would have smiled and offered to help clean him up. She would have been happy he'd returned home. And she would have set aside all of the lingering heartache from their last and supposedly final breakup.

But too much time had slipped past. Too much had changed. And for him to show up now? In the middle of the night when her fear rose to fever pitch? For him to waltz in here without even knocking?

She felt Caroline's hand close around her arm and pull as if trying to drag her away. Lily grabbed her wine glass and hurled it at the door. She missed and the glass fell to the ground three feet in front of her and shattered.

"Turn around and leave, Dominic," she snapped as she allowed Caroline to pull her behind the bar, into relative safety. Only she'd never be safe from the man she'd loved for so long, because he didn't aim for her face or her arms.

He went for the heart.

"You had your chance to come back," she added as Caroline released her.

"Lily, please calm down," Dominic called.

From their position behind the bar, she heard the door close. Caroline glanced at her. "You know him."

She nodded. Caroline pushed off the ground without a word. And Lily followed her, turning to face the former love of her life, who had stepped just inside the door.

"Ryan dragged me back," he said. "At Noah and Josie's request. How do you think I got the key? Or does your friend here throw food at everyone who walks into the bar?"

"It was the only thing I had," Caroline said simply. "Noah locked up my gun."

"Remind me to thank Noah in the morning," Dominic said dryly.

His hands dropped to his side, abandoning the attempts to wipe away the pie that had hit its target with near-perfect aim. Lily glanced at Caroline. She wasn't sure she wanted to see the dishwasher with a firearm.

Then she glanced back at Dominic. Marionberries clung to his beard. He'd always been clean-shaven. But now, his dark hair was long and it looked like he'd lost his razor around the same time he'd kissed the rangers goodbye. She'd loved the hard lines of his jaw and the feel of his skin against her when they kissed. But this look . . .

She ached to touch and explore. He looked wild and unrestrained, as if he didn't give a damn, as if he didn't hold anything back. Her gaze headed south to the muscles she'd wanted to memorize before he left. He appeared bigger, more powerful.

Impossible.

He'd always been strong, able to lift her up and press her against the wall. He'd held her with ease while she fell apart . . .

And with that memory, her fury and her fear opened the door to another entirely unwelcome emotion—desire. It was as if they were forming a club determined to barricade her heart, mind, and soul against the feelings that might help her return to her calm, steady life. But no, her unruly emotions took one look at the bearded, buff man in the bar and thought: *touch him!*

Her feelings needed to shut the hell up, she thought as she stared at him. "Dominic, why are you here?" Lily asked. "Why did they *make you* come back?"

"To keep you safe."

"You refused to come home after you were discharged, after you couldn't serve. But now you show up because Josie and Noah claim I need a bodyguard?"

He raised his right hand to his beard as if to remove the berries and then thought better of it. "Lily—"

"Did they tell you that the police, including your father, think I was in the wrong place at the wrong time?" she demanded. "Did Ryan explain how everyone else believes he was just some crazy person who wanted to slash my face to leave scars . . ."

Her voice broke as his familiar green eyes shone with pity at her words.

"Yes," he said simply. "Ryan told me."

"So you came back to protect me from what exactly?" she said, hating that he looked at her as if she'd given in to fear. "My own shadow? The man out to get me that no one believes exists?"

He nodded.

No, no, no! I refuse to let him back into my life now.

"Well, if everyone is so damn concerned about me, if everyone thinks I need a bodyguard—"

"It's not like that," he said firmly. "They're worried and they want you to feel safe. It doesn't matter if someone is out there or not. If you don't feel safe, if you need someone to stand guard outside your house and watch the doors, make sure no one is climbing in the windows . . . I can do that."

Lily let out a laugh. After all this time, after all her attempts to build a future with this man, he'd come back to patrol her street. But she wanted a false sense of security about as much as she wanted empty promises.

I'll try to make it work, Lil. I promise.

But then he'd deploy with his rangers and send an email listing a bunch of bullshit reasons why she was better off without him. And then after he'd been shot . . .

I'm no good for you, Lil. Look at me. I'm all busted up. I don't want you wasting your life taking care of me. You've done that once. I won't let you do it again.

Well, now she was broken too. And she refused to let him waste his time watching out for a threat he didn't believe existed.

No, she wanted security. She needed to feel safe to move through her life, knowing they'd identified and caught her assailant. But Dominic Fairmore was nothing more than a quick fix that would offer a false refuge only to pull it away. She couldn't trust him to stay, to help her, or to believe her.

"If I need a bodyguard, I choose her," Lily said, pointing to the woman who wore combat boots to clean dishes. "I want the woman who knows how to throw a pie at my supposedly nonexistent bogeyman."

Chapter Four

DOMINIC LICKED HIS lips. He could taste the sugar from
the pie and recognized the Oregon berry. Hell, it was like
being assaulted with a blast from his past as soon as he
arrived in town. Ryan had shoved him off the red-eye
flight, directed him to the car rental counter, and handed
him the key to Noah's bar. Then his childhood friend had
boarded a flight home to the air force base.

And Dominic had driven back in time. He could
practically hear his mom laughing as he licked the bowl.
The smell of fresh pie used to fill the farmhouse kitchen
once upon a time. And then one day it had stopped. His
mother had succumbed to a heart condition no one knew
she had, leaving behind a son who wanted to make damn
sure he left his mark on the world before his life was cut
short.

Yeah, one helluva mark.

He glanced down at his injured hand. He'd tried to wipe the food from his face and his damn fingers had failed to comb through his beard.

He looked up at Lily, his eyes searching for the scars. He wanted to see what that bastard had done to her. But her long blond hair caught his attention and new memories swirled to life. His hands wrapped in her long locks . . . pulling her head back as he pressed into her from behind . . .

Fuck.

He looked away and fought to control the unwelcome need rushing through him. But this was Lily, the only woman he'd ever made love to, the only woman he'd craved since he was a teenager Though if he added up Lily's desire to have the petite dark-haired woman protect her, the one who had used a pie as a weapon simply because she couldn't shoot him, and the fact that Lily had tried to hit him with her wine glass, he could quickly reach the conclusion that her feelings didn't mirror his.

Lily wanted him gone. She didn't want his help. And he'd bet that if he tried to touch her, she would throw something else at him. He didn't want to think about what she'd do if he attempted to revisit that place where he could sink into her and love her.

Beating back his desire, he stole another glance at her face. This time he spotted the proof that someone had taken a knife to her. A thin line ran down her cheek. It was fading, but still visible. He knew other cut marks lay beneath her long-sleeve crew-neck shirt. Behind the picture of the old mechanical Big Buck's bull across her torso, one slash had come close to tearing up her stomach and hitting her internal organs. Ryan had filled him in on the details on the flight.

He looked up, straight into her beautiful blue eyes. There was a ferocity there that threatened to break him. She was still so damn beautiful. But the sweet innocence was gone. And he didn't see a trace of the playful humor she'd reserved for him.

Or maybe someone else now. . .

His jaw tightened and he swallowed in an attempt to beat back the jealousy. He'd lived with it on and off for years, telling himself she was better off with someone who wasn't hell-bent on being a soldier first and a man second.

But if she had someone, where the hell was he? Why was she eating pie in a closed bar in the middle of the night?

"No," the other woman said, shattering the taut silence. "I can't. I can't keep anyone safe. Not when I still . . . I can't."

"Caroline, I wasn't asking," Lily said. "I just need him to leave."

The other woman—Caroline—took a step back and moved to the side of the bar. "Let's call Noah."

Lily nodded as if this was a good idea.

"No," he said. "Don't bother him now. It's the middle of the night. I'll go. But I'm not leaving town. I'll be out there, watching over you, Lily. I'll stay in my car and patrol the street. So you go on home and lock your doors. And tonight, try to get some sleep. Because no one is getting past me."

"You're going to sleep in your car?" she said.

"I didn't say anything about sleep." He stole combat naps, but never sleep. Then tomorrow when she went to work, he'd talk to Noah, his dad—anyone who might be able to help him find the son of a bitch who'd hurt her. He didn't care if her assailant had targeted her or not— Dominic was going to make damn sure Lily knew the bastard would never hurt her again. "But I'm not leaving you, Lil. Not until I know you feel safe."

"You don't really believe there's a threat out there," she said, her eyes narrowing.

He studied the woman he saw every damn time he closed his eyes. Beneath her work shirt and jeans, she still possessed curves designed to bring his need to a boiling point. She looked the same apart from the still-angry slash marks. But he could see from here that she didn't feel the same.

That makes two of us.

"It doesn't matter what I believe," he said. "How you feel—that's all I give a damn about."

She let out a sharp bark of laughter. "Now you choose to care about my feelings?"

He nodded. What the hell could he say? That he wanted the world for her? That he always had? But he'd never been the guy to put her first and he damn well knew it. And now, he was a broken mess.

"I'm going to find him, Lil. The man who hurt you." He turned to the door and pulled it open. "I'll be in my car whenever you're ready to head home."

DOMINIC REACHED FOR the mega-sized coffee cup and came up empty. He'd run out just as the sun was high in the Oregon sky. But he had feeling Lily wouldn't wake up anytime soon. Sure, they'd driven to her quiet cul-de-sac not long after the pie-throwing incident in the bar. But she'd spent the next hour or so walking through her house, turning lights on and off as if she needed to check behind every door.

And then she'd fallen asleep with the curtains pulled open, her hand resting on the windowsill, and her face turned toward him.

He hadn't moved since. Sure, he could use a nap. And he needed to wash the berry pie out of his beard once he got out of this car. Positioning the empty coffee cup back in the holder, he shifted in his seat. The baby-blue rental sedan felt cramped compared to the truck he'd left behind in Georgia.

He'd thought about coming home a time or ten. He'd debated asking his dad for a job with the police force. Only he couldn't shoot. Maybe one day, with more physical therapy . . . but that day had moved further and further away as his physical therapy stagnated. The nerves in his hand refused to respond. So he'd stopped going. He'd given up.

With the way the sunlight hit her bedroom window, he couldn't see inside. He could picture the pink walls. He'd peered inside once. Of course, her mother had hovered nearby to make damn sure he kept his feet planted firmly in the hall. But he'd glanced enough to know her walls matched her favorite nail polish color. And just thinking about those pink toes . . .

He glanced down at his lap and willed himself not to feel a thing. He couldn't want her. They'd traveled down that road and hit too many dead ends. She'd built a life here. And his had taken him to places he didn't want to remember. He'd fought through nightmares, so damn determined to make it all worthwhile, until one man with a gun had stripped away his sense of purpose.

And if they couldn't make their relationship work when he was something—a soldier, a ranger—Lily wouldn't want him now. Even if they got past her desire to hurl things at him for daring to come home to watch over her, he had a feeling she'd still be pissed he hadn't shown up years earlier looking for her heart.

Knock.

His head turned to the passenger side window and his gaze locked on Lily. She'd exchanged her work clothes for black athletic shorts and a hot-pink long-sleeve top. Her blond hair hung in a long ponytail down her back, and in her hands, she held two steaming mugs.

He leaned across the car's center console and opened the passenger side door. "You're up early," he murmured.

"Coming from the man who I'm guessing never closed

his eyes last night." She handed him a mug. "I thought you might need a cup of coffee. It's black. I haven't gone grocery shopping in a while, so no milk."

"Thank you." He accepted the cup with his good hand and raised it to his lips. After his first sip, he nodded to the passenger seat. "Care to join me?"

She climbed into the car, her own mug gripped between her hands. "You can't live in your car, Dominic. The neighbors will call the cops eventually."

"My dad is eager to see me, but I doubt he'll arrest me," he said mildly. Having her here, so close, after a long night of watching her sleep and wanting her no matter how much he tried to deny it sent mixed signals to his tired body. And yeah, most of those instructions headed below the belt. He shifted again.

"Your father's missed you." She raised her mug and sipped her coffee. "I'm wondering, what did Ryan have to do to drag you back here? Hog-tie you?"

He said your name.

But now, after she'd welcomed him by hurling things at him, probably wasn't the best time to tell her he still had feelings for her. She'd probably toss her hot coffee at him if he sat here and explained that he planned to channel his emotions into playing bodyguard.

"I'd never let that happen," he said.

She cocked her head and looked right at him. "That's what was missing from our relationship. You never let me tie you up."

He drank in her sarcastic tone. Then he let out a laugh and shook his head. "That's going to stay in your wildest fantasies, honey. But I'm sure as . . . sure happy you're still joking around after everything."

"No, not really," she murmured, her voice flat and humorless now. "Not anymore."

"Lil, you can't let that bastard take that away from you. You can't move on, shake the memories if—"

"Your dad thinks I'm safe," she said. "The guy from the park—he's not after me. And he never was."

"But you don't agree."

"You ruined everything."

Well shit, that pretty much summed it up, didn't it?

And he knew it wasn't because he'd never let her bind him to the bedposts and have her way with him.

"That's what he said," she continued. "When he attacked me. And those words, his voice . . . it felt personal."

"You shared this with my dad?" He worked to keep his tone neutral and not jump to conclusions based on things he shouldn't feel for her after all this time.

She nodded. "But all the evidence suggests that he was crazy. That this was a random attack. He didn't even take my phone." She lifted her gaze and looked through the front windshield. "I *know* it was personal."

"I believe you." And hell, he meant it. The Lily he'd known in high school, the girl he'd fallen in love with, the woman who'd cared for her mother when her dad couldn't handle his wife's illness—she was strong. She wouldn't give in to fear without a reason.

"I'll talk to my dad," he continued. "And until we find him, I don't mind watching the stars from my car. Though I'm kicking myself for not driving my truck up here. Ryan was so damn determined to get me on that plane."

"You're really staying this time." Her lips pressed to the rim of her cup.

"Until we find the guy." *And until you feel like you can fall asleep without checking every corner of your house.*

"Then you're leaving again. To do what?"

"I'll figure something out," he said. Or he'd spend the rest of his days with his feet resting on a damn box, drinking coffee and staring at his TV. Worthless. Useless. A failure. And sure as hell not worthy of the woman sitting beside him.

"You want to lick your wounds someplace else, away from your family."

He turned and looked into her blue eyes. "I'm not getting any better. The damage is done. And no, I don't know where to go from here. Hell, if I drank something stronger than coffee, I'd probably lose myself in a drunken haze—"

"No, you wouldn't," she said. "I've never met a man more determined to act, who refused to settle. Life is too short, remember? You said it all the time."

"Looks like 'life' had the last laugh," he muttered. "Because it sure as shit broke me."

"Not all of you, I hope," she said.

"Lily." And yeah, his tone held a shitload of warning. If she glanced below the belt and teased him with her words . . .

"You can tell me. Because I get it. Life broke me too," she said. "But I'm fighting back. I accepted Noah's job offer because I knew I needed to get out of the house. I can't hide forever. School starts again at the end of August. I need to be able to face a roomful of five-year-olds. Lead them. Teach them. And not rush off to the bathroom and hide because I can't overcome the panic."

Dominic took a long sip of the now warm coffee. He'd fought with dozens of men who wore their bravery like body armor. And he'd been one of them until he'd been hit. Then he'd crumbled. If Ryan hadn't shown up, he'd still be hiding from the world instead of helping a woman who made army rangers look like pansies.

"Planning to follow me everywhere?" she asked, breaking the silence.

"Yeah."

"OK then. Today's my day off. I'm going back inside to do a workout video. And then, I have a date later. So try not to peer in the windows."

I have a date later.

No longer awestruck by her determination to get back to the kids who needed her, he turned those words over. Lily was too damn special to remain single. And she'd given him plenty of chances. But still . . .

"Take the mug," he said.

"You're done?" she asked.

"I don't want to break it."

"Is your hand hurting?" Her brow furrowed as she accepted the mug.

No, honey. That's my fucking heart, which came close to stopping once in the middle of a terrorist camp . . . and now here.

He wanted to take her concern and bottle it up. But that desire pretty much summed up why he hadn't come home to her.

"Something like that." He needed to get a grip on his emotions. "He's coming over? Your date?"

She nodded. And yeah, it was a damn good thing he'd handed back the mug. He'd have coffee splattered all over his lap right now and his good hand would be sliced to pieces from the ceramic if he hadn't returned it to her care.

"What does he look like?"

Her blue eyes narrowed as she gripped both mugs. "Why?"

"I don't want to hurt him by mistake," he said. "If he shows up, knocks on your door, hell, I might think he's here to hurt you."

"Ted runs the elementary school literacy program," she said. "He's tall, slim, and has blond hair. And his smile . . ."

Fuck Ted's smile.

"Yeah?" he said.

"When he smiles, he looks sweet and kind," she added.

Thank God in heaven, her tone suggested sweetness should be reserved for the coffee in her cup.

"Does he laugh at your jokes?" he demanded.

"He doesn't find me funny," she said. "But—"

"And he sure as shit doesn't make you feel safe," he said. "Or he'd be by your side night and day, making sure no one hurts you."

"He trusts the police and thinks I'm overreacting. What happened was awful, but it's over. Done. I should move on. And I am . . ."

It's not that easy. You'll never be the same. Even if you prove that you're right and the police are wrong.

But now probably wasn't the time to tell her that. She'd figure it out on her own.

"Ted is a good man," she said. "He's great with kids."

But is he good with you? Does he know how to make you come, make you scream with pleasure while he buries his face between your legs?

Dominic wasn't that guy. Not anymore, but he knew what she deserved.

"Maybe you should ask him to wear a sign when he comes to pick you up that reads 'Ted, the Good Guy,'" he said.

She smiled, but her blue eyes shone with challenge. It was as if he'd told her he couldn't keep seeing her all over again. Until that last time, when he'd been free and clear of his duty to serve, she'd never demanded that he change his mind.

"He'll probably show up with flowers," she said, thrusting his mug back into his hand. Then she reached for the door.

"Is that why you and your partner in crime hurled pie and wine at me last night?" he asked mildly. "Because I forgot the flowers?"

"Once upon a time, you showed up with Chinese take-out when you know I hate everything about it," she said.

You have one helluva memory. But then he recalled the color of her nail polish and the way the light played off her pink toes.

"I've never expected flowers from you," she continued, thrusting the door open. "I never expected you to come back here."

He held up his damaged right hand. "I'm broken—"

"So you've what, been throwing yourself an extended pity party?"

"Yeah. But I didn't want guests," he said, his gaze fixed on the ugly scar in the center of his palm. "I needed time to put my life back together before I showed up here. I had to come to terms with the fact that I threw away a helluva lot to end up on the sidelines with a fucking hand that won't work. A bullet nicked my pulmonary artery and it's the one that passed through my hand that left me unable to serve, to hold a gun, to shave my face like I could before."

He looked over at her and his gaze honed in on the visible reminders of her attack slashed across her skin. He'd spent the night watching over the kindergarten teacher who'd proven far more resilient. He'd spent months hiding from the uncertainty of his future. But she'd gone out, weeks after her attack, and started working again. She'd pushed out of her comfort zone, determined to get to back to her classroom.

"And now you can't go back to who you were before," she said.

"I can still keep you safe," he promised.

"Because you don't believe there is a threat out there. You think it's all in my head."

"I didn't say that," he ground out. "I—"

"You didn't need to." She shifted her legs and climbed out of the car. Then she turned back and said, "You're promising to keep me safe, but you just admitted you can't even fire a gun."

He watched her walk away and wondered if he'd made a mistake coming back. He should have told Ryan to fly back and talk to her new boyfriend. He should be the one picking up the slack here. But if Ted with the flowers was such a great guy, why wasn't he out here making damn sure she felt safe while she slept?

Because Ted didn't believe her.

"I believe you, Lily," he said, his words filling the now empty sedan. "If you say the bastard was after you, then he was. And I don't need a gun to keep you safe. I can take care of you. Just don't expect me to bring you a bunch of fucking flowers."

Chapter Five

"WHERE'S MY BROTHER?" Josie demanded as she shifted her weight from side to side to calm the nine-month-old baby strapped to her chest. The little girl's big green eyes peered over the edge of the carrier. She opened her mouth and bit down on the fabric edge, then smiled.

"I sent Dominic home to shower," Lily said. Her gaze shifted away from the bundle of cuteness to Noah, who was pretending to count beer cases. Unless sleep deprivation prevented him from reaching the magical number four, Big Buck's owner and manager knew exactly how many cases of light beer were stacked beside the long wooden bar.

"I thought you called me in on my day off so that Noah could teach me how to mix up a martini," she said. "Are customers complaining? Missing their fancy drinks? Or are we expecting James Bond?"

"We stopped by Noah's dad's house this morning and

Caroline filled us in on Dominic's arrival," Josie said. "From what she said, I thought my brother was taking his role to watch over you seriously."

"He is. But after sleeping in his car covered in pie, I'm guessing he needed a shower. Plus, I thought your dad would like to see him. But don't worry, Dominic promised to be back on the job for my date with Ted tonight."

Five feet away, Noah dropped the clipboard onto the polished floorboards.

"I didn't realize you and Ted were still together," Josie said. She stopped her rocking motions and leaned back against one of the high-top tables near the bar.

"Or you wouldn't have sent Ryan to bring your brother home?" she asked.

Noah abandoned his failed attempt to complete the inventory. "Lily—"

"When you offered me a temporary job, I didn't realize it came with a bodyguard," she said, unleashing her frustration. They had no right to step in and throw another curve ball into her life, not when it felt like she was holding it together with Scotch tape and paperclips. "Or is that part of the Big Buck's benefits package? Did you arrange for Josh and his pies too? Is that how you make Caroline feel safe? Is Josh Summers her Big Buck's–ordered bodyguard?"

"No." The firm, familiar voice cut through the bar. "No. That's not why Josh brings pies."

Lily turned to the swinging door that led to the Employees Only space. They hadn't flipped the sign out front to "Open until the cows come home," but Big Buck's dishwasher had her own key to the place and permission to enter through the back room.

"I'd stop Josh if I could," Noah muttered. "But he's more stubborn than the trees he fells."

"We're friends," Caroline said. But Lily could see the hint of doubt in the other woman's eyes.

"Josh's brothers are tired of eating his pies so he brings them here," Caroline continued. "Baking helps with his memory. He was in a logging accident a while back. He was hit in the head and lost his short-term memory."

"If he just needs to keep his mind sharp, he could pick up Sudoku," Noah muttered.

"There are some fears not even you can protect me from, Noah," Caroline said simply.

Noah sighed. "Yeah, I've received that message loud and clear."

Lily studied the woman she'd asked to act as her bodyguard last night. Caroline seemed so bold, ready to jump into action, throwing pies or shooting guns. What was she afraid of?

"Did it help? Having Dominic parked outside?" Josie asked, steering the conversation away from her mysterious coworker.

"Yes." Lily headed for the front door leading to the parking area. "But I'm not sure it's good for him. If he wanted to be here, he would have come home a while ago."

"Sometimes it's hard to think of home as the best place to lick your wounds," Josie said softly.

And Lily knew she spoke from experience. Once upon a time, Josie Fairmore had been Forever's bad girl. She'd left. And she'd stayed away even when she needed help. Lily didn't know the full story. But she'd heard enough.

"Josie, I know you think that maybe he will stay for me. But I don't want him to," Lily said flatly. "I'm not interested in being his consolation prize. I don't want him camped outside my front door, thinking 'I could be out there freeing the world from terrorists, but instead I'm helping my ex-girlfriend face her supposedly imaginary fears.' I don't need him making the dark a little less scary."

Liar.

Because I know the threat is still out there.

"Now if you don't mind saving your drink lessons for another day," Lily said, opening the door, "I need to paint my nails and get ready for my date."

LILY CLOSED HER front door behind the man she would never marry and turned the lock. She stared at her burgundy-red nails.

I should have learned how to make a martini instead. Shaken, not stirred.

Or maybe she'd prefer the hard liquor swirled together? She didn't know and she wasn't about to find out. Because tonight she planned to drown her sorrows in wine the color of her fingernails.

She headed for the bottle-lined rack that she'd added to her parents' living room after her mother passed away and her father moved out. The top shelf held a selection of Oregon pinot noirs from a "girlfriends" winery tour she'd taken with some of her fellow teachers.

Those same friends had slipped away, retreating into their own busy lives after she'd been attacked. Oh, they'd helped at first, dropping off food and staying to talk for a while. But they'd stopped calling as the summer went on and she stayed at home, more and more convinced someone would hurt her.

Except Noah and Josie. They'd practically broken down the door to talk to her. But they hadn't wanted to make small talk. Noah and Josie had offered her a job. They'd begged for her help. Pour beer. Open wine bottles. Offer shots. Maybe mix a simple drink or two while Noah's regular part-time bartender took a two-week trip to Hawaii. Not one mention of tossing Dominic into the mix.

She withdrew a bottle and headed for the archway leading to the kitchen.

Knock. Knock.

She froze, her grip tightening around the bottle's neck. She could use it to hit the person on the other side of the door over the head . . .

"I know you're in there," Dominic's deep voice called. "I saw your date arrive and then leave again without you."

She sighed and crossed the short entryway. Then she removed the chain, flipped the deadbolt, and opened the door a foot.

"Is he coming back?" Dominic asked, eyeing the bottle in her hand.

"No."

"Family emergency?"

She shook her head from side to side.

He folded his arms in front of his broad chest. The stance put his biceps on display, which was nice . . . but she really needed the wine first. Maybe after a glass or two, she would ask him to take off his shirt so that she could admire his muscles. She wouldn't touch. That would remind her of the man attached to those biceps. The man she refused to forgive for staying away so long. Still, it would be nice to have a drink and look—

"Let me guess, Good Guy Ted took one look at your curled hair, freshly painted nails, and sinful dress, and he decided to make a run for it so that he didn't embarrass himself? Looking at you, there's no way he wanted to walk away."

"Sinful dress?" she muttered. "It covers my arms and practically reaches my knee."

"But you're wearing it," he said, making a show of looking her up and down.

She shifted her weight from one bare foot to the other. The dress didn't exactly hide the extra five pounds she hadn't bothered to work off since her last jogging disaster. Her hips felt full beneath the fabric. Her breasts pressed up against her bra as if they might try to escape.

The dress will hide your injuries.

That had been her sole criteria when she'd plucked it from her closet, intending to wear it for Ted. But now that Dominic was scrutinizing her, she started thinking about how her body felt beneath the dress.

Full. Hot. Needy.

"And for the record," he added, "it's not the dress that I like, it's what's beneath."

"Fine, you can come in," she said as if every compliment had been a fishing line cast out hoping to reel in an invitation. The alternative—that he meant every word, that he still thought she was beautiful . . . No, she'd rather pretend he'd been trying to secure an invite to sleep on her couch instead of in his car.

"I was just about to pour a glass of wine and run the wildflowers that Ted bought at the grocery store down the garbage disposal," she added as he stepped into the entryway.

"And you wonder why I never brought you flowers," he said, taking over the task of locking the door and replacing the chain.

She held up the bottle. "Would you like a glass? I don't have beer. And I have no idea how to mix a martini."

"How about coffee?" He walked forward, glancing through the archway off the living room that led to the kitchen.

"It's late." She followed him into the bright yellow kitchen that made her think of sunshine and summer. Before summer had become connected to violence. "It might keep you up."

"That's the plan."

He headed straight for the coffeemaker as if he knew his way around. But that was impossible. She'd replaced the cabinets and countertops. Every appliance had been ripped out and redone. The construction ate up most of her savings, but it had been worth it to make the place her own, not a part leftover from her parents' lives.

"I'm not much use to you if I'm asleep," he added. "Instead of keeping a lookout."

She exhaled as if she'd been holding that particular breath for a week, maybe more. He'd be out there tonight, watching over her. She would be safe for one more night.

"What happened with your boyfriend?" he asked once the machine sputtered to life and started gurgling.

She turned away, focusing on the drawer that held the wine opener. "He's no longer mine." She fished the corkscrew out and set about trying to open the bottle. "He ended it."

"Jesus, Lily." He spoke from behind her. And then his hand covered hers on the bottle. He gently pulled it away from her and finished the job with his left hand. Then he held it out to her. "You're really racking up a list of men I need to hunt down and hurt."

She took the wine and turned away. She needed a glass before she took a long, deep swig straight from the source. And if she did that, he'd never believe . . .

"I'm not upset," she muttered, opening the cabinet and removing a glass tumbler. She didn't need stemware tonight. "The mugs are over the coffeemaker."

Carrying her filled glass, she headed for the living room. The small, tidy space held her father's old baby-blue recliner, a three-person sofa covered in worn brown leather, and a wooden coffee table that her mother had purchased at a yard sale. Matching side tables stood at either end of the couch and the entire set looked as if it had been handmade by one of the local loggers. But the hunting lodge motif looked out of place in the small two-bedroom one-story house.

A mechanical sound emanated from the kitchen, drawing her attention away from the furnishing she should probably update at some point. It continued for a moment, the grinding noise chased by the rush of running water. And then it stopped.

"Trouble finding a mug?" she called. Any other night, the noise would have launched her into a panic. But Dominic was here now. She could save her hide-under-the-covers instinct for another night.

"Nah." He walked into the room holding an "I Love My Teacher" mug. "I was disposing of your flowers for you."

"Thank you," she murmured, tracking his movements as he bypassed the recliner and claimed the other end of the sofa.

"Do you always keep the curtains open?" He nodded to the drapes pulled back to reveal a sliding glass door leading to the outside.

"Not at first," she said. "But my imagination ran wild, wondering who might be on the other side."

He nodded as if her fears made perfect sense. "Would more light out there help? Maybe a camera or two?"

"It might." She stared out into the darkness. "There's one light set up on a motion sensor. I thought floodlights would annoy the neighbors."

"They'll adjust." He set his mug on the nearest side table. "Why did Ted break up with you?"

"Because I leave the curtains open," she said and he raised an eyebrow. But she knew he understood her words. This had nothing to do with concerns about Peeping Toms spying on them in the bedroom.

Not that she'd slept with Ted. Well, maybe Dominic didn't need to know that piece.

"And because I can't stop wondering where he is," she added. "Not Ted, but—"

"The man who attacked you," he said.

"Yes. I want to know why he did it and when he'll come back." She gulped her wine to keep her voice from wavering over the last word.

"And Tom wanted what? Rainbows and sunshine?"

"Ted," she corrected. "And he wanted kids. He's ready to settle down, not coach me through 'the aftermath.' Plus, I think the cuts scared him."

"He didn't like your injuries? It looks to me like they'll heal without much scarring. I can't even see the one on your face." Dominic's voice was a low rumble. His gaze drifted lower, probably imagining the horrors hiding beneath her dress and wondering if their mutual friends had lied about the extent of her injures.

"Makeup," she said. "And they're not that bad. The one on my side is the deepest. But Ted never saw that one."

His relief was palpable as he leaned forward and rested his arms on his thighs.

"But Ted has a reputation for fainting over a paper cut," she added. "So even the mostly healed wounds on my face and arms were too much for him."

His expression hardened. Add in his new beard and

longer hair and Dominic now appeared downright menacing. "You know, I'm not very accurate," he said slowly. "But I can still get off a round or two with a pistol. Where did you say Tom lives?"

"Ted. And I didn't." She raised her glass to her lips. After all this time, all the anger she'd steered his way for not coming back, why did his jealousy feel so welcome?

"One more question," he said.

She nodded, hoping he'd tack on another after that. She wasn't ready for him to leave her alone in the house surrounded by dark corners. His presence filled her space. It stole her concentration away from the what-ifs that usually followed her around. What if someone jumped out at her again? What if there was someone hiding in her closet? Or behind her shower curtain?

"Why the hell did you paint your nails for him?" Dominic demanded.

Maybe it was the wine, or the possessive gleam in his green eyes, or his familiar presence, but she decided to give him the honest answer. Though she knew it might lead them down a path she wasn't sure she wanted to travel again. But one that just might keep him in her home awhile longer.

"Well," she murmured. "They had to match my panties."

GODDAMN IT, I'VE missed her mouth.

Dominic cocked his head, hoping like hell she planned to down the entire bottle of wine. Not because he wanted to take advantage. No, he wanted an excuse to look at her a little longer. Her blond ringlets danced over her shoulders, teasing her dress's modest scoop neckline. The garment he'd labeled "sinful" hugged her curves in a way that confirmed Good Guy Ted was an idiot. Add in her smart mouth and how the hell could Ted walk away from her?

How dare Mr. Good Guy leave her knowing she's afraid of the dark and every corner of the house she grew up in? I should hunt him down and hurt him for that alone.

"Prove it," he said, his tone level and even, as if he wouldn't trade the use of his good hand to see her panties right now. "Show me what you wearing beneath that dress. Not because I brought you flowers—"

"You didn't. And you ran the ones I had down the disposal."

"Show me," he ordered, a smile playing on his lips at her sharp retort.

Dominic waited for her anger to rise up and surpass her fears. Any second now, she'd send him back to his rental car. Probably after she demanded to know where he got off asking for a view he'd refused to come home to for so long. If he was lucky, she'd let him keep the coffee.

She drained her glass and set it on the coffee table. "I'll show you my underwear if you lose your shirt."

Chapter Six

DOMINIC REACHED BEHIND his head and tugged on his T-shirt. The rising fabric revealed his abdomen. And yeah, he liked the way her gaze followed the hemline. But his arm stilled, his bicep taut and his T-shirt covering his hair. If he kept going, she'd see the damaged skin on his chest from where the bullet had entered.

"Are you sure about this?" he asked. "My scars aren't pretty."

"I promise to focus on your abs," she murmured without looking up. "And lower."

He laughed as he pulled the shirt over his head and tossed it aside. Lily had never offered pity before. Why should she start now? No, the curve of her lips and excitement in her blue eyes suggested she'd take what she wanted from him. She wouldn't hold back.

She never holds back. That's me. I'm the one fighting this pull with everything I have in me.

He'd walked away from her over and over. He'd told himself it was the right thing to do. Be brave. Fight for freedom. Make your mark on this world while you still can. He'd buffered his heartbreak with good and noble intentions. Only to be sidelined by bullets. It was as if the enemy had won, taking him out before he'd done enough. And now he didn't have a clue how to find his way forward.

Lily.

No, he was pretty damn certain he wouldn't find his future staring at Lily's panties. Plus, she was living day to day right now. She didn't need his bullshit heaped on top of her struggles.

He shouldn't look. Hell, he should stand up and walk out of here now. He'd done what he came to do—check on her. He'd come home to keep her safe. And he had to draw the line there. After all she'd been through he couldn't drag her back into heartbreak.

He was leaving. That was a fact. He refused to stay in Forever and lick his wounds.

"My turn now," she said.

Her red nails toyed with the hem of her skirt. One manicured hand held the fabric down while the other drew a small section of her dress up to her thighs. She reached the thin band of burgundy circling her hips.

"See," she said, holding her fingers over the splash of color against her pale skin. "They match."

Dominic stared at the elastic band as if he'd been ordered to memorize the details. But this wasn't a reconnaissance mission. He wouldn't be returning to see how

her underwear looked from the back, her skirt pulled up
to her hips . . .

I bet it's a thong.

Desire raged like a spreading flame. But on its heels?
A big green monster. He thought of the flowers in the disposal and the selfish bastard who'd left them behind.

"I don't think Ted deserves panties like those," he
growled.

"And you do?" she asked coyly.

"Probably not."

"If I let go with my right hand, my dress will probably
rise up higher. Maybe to my waist."

"It might." He lifted his gaze to her face. Her blue
eyes shone with daring, but also a hint of desperation.
Was that why she was sitting there, teasing him? Was she
trying to stave off emotions she'd rather not feel? Trying
to keep him here just so she wouldn't be alone?

"Don't do it," he added. "Not now. Not tonight."

The red-tipped fingers holding her dress up at her hip
let go and the fabric slipped back into place. He watched
it trail over her thighs, leaving him so damn jealous of
her fucking clothes. He wanted to touch her. But that
was nothing new. He'd spent years waking up in foreign
countries and dreaming about her soft skin against his.

He reached for his coffee and tried to find the right
words.

I want to fuck you on your coffee table.

While that had a ring of truth to it, he couldn't put
that out there. Not when he knew she needed a helluva lot

more than a quickie in her living room. Sure, they could both lose themselves in the pleasure for a while. He'd dreamed about doing just that, finding some random chick for a night, to ease the pain as he came to terms with his future and his fears.

But he refused to be Lily's escape. Not when he could be her way through this mess.

"Tell me how you feel, Lily."

"Like someone just stole away my chance for an orgasm tonight," she said.

"Look at me." He waited for her eyes to meet his. Her lips parted as she obeyed. And he studied her expression. But dammit, he couldn't pinpoint what drove her to offer a view of her underwear, to let him in, to wake up and try to get through the day. He could guess, but . . .

Once upon a time, before the sharp edge of reality stripped away the fairy tale, he'd been able to read her. He'd soothed her sadness. He'd held her while she wept after her mother's diagnosis. But now?

"Talk to me," he said. "You used to tell me everything. About your mom. Your dad . . ."

Her eyes narrowed. "I did. You're the only one who knew what it cost me to watch my mother suffer and know there was nothing I could do to save her. You know how hard it was to see my dad slip deeper and deeper into addiction. I turned to you when I realized I couldn't save him. I shared everything I was feeling. And then you walked away, taking pieces of me with you."

"I'm sorry," he said. And damn, he hoped she could

see the truth in his face, because the words felt inadequate. Apologies didn't fix the past. He couldn't make amends with words.

"I hated you for a while." She glanced down at her hands clasped tight in her lap. "But it doesn't feel good to hold a grudge against the man who left to hunt down terrorists. It's like wishing rainstorms on the people standing on the shores to welcome the refugees."

"You have every right to hate me for not coming home after they released me from the hospital."

"True." She looked up, but didn't return her gaze to his face. She stared out the sliding doors and into the night. "But I'm starting to realize . . . fear isn't easy. It's not something you can set aside at bedtime. I wish I could most nights."

"I wasn't afraid," he said. "I was stupid."

Now, she turned to face him and raised an eyebrow.

"OK, maybe a bit of both," he admitted. "To tell you the truth, I'm still scared."

"Of the dark?" she asked in a tone that called BS to his claim.

"No, honey. I don't mind the dark." It was his turn to look away. He hadn't shared his feelings with anyone in a long time. The military shrink he'd tried to convince that he was fine and ready to serve again—that guy didn't count.

"I'm afraid I'll never be of much use to anyone," he continued. Why hide the truth from her? She deserved to know why he couldn't stay here staring at the pieces of his previous life. "I feel too damn broken. I thought I knew what my future held. I walked away from this place, from you, determined to make that sacrifice matter. And to suddenly be out of the game? I feel like a fucking failure, Lil. And I don't think that will change if I stay here."

He waited for her to envelop him in a hug and shower him with comforting words. And hell, if Lily shoveled on the pity now . . . it sure as shit would erase the last trace of his desire.

"Well, I'm scared of the dark," she said as if he hadn't just poured out his heart and soul. "I'm afraid to close my eyes. Even when I'm in the shower, I'm terrified to wash my hair because I'll have to close my eyes for a split second. And that's all it takes. He could get into my house and . . . I know he's out there. It wasn't a random attack."

Oh, Lily. His heart broke for her.

"I'm afraid to go out alone. And I'm terrified to stay in by myself," she said, the words pouring out one after the other, faster and faster. "You want to know how I feel? Paralyzed by fear. And I hate him. Whoever he is, I hate him for doing this to me."

I'm going to kill him. When I get my hands on the man who did this. . .

She let out a bark of laughter. "Hate and fear. That's my life. Is it any wonder that I want to add an orgasm to the mix?"

"No, it's not surprising. But I'm not your guy."

She shook her head. "There's never been anyone else. Not for me. And that scares me too."

Reach for her. Pull her close. Kiss her.

His mind issued the commands in rapid-fire succession. His body responded to those words. And his hands moved. He set the coffee mug on the table and . . .

No, he couldn't touch her. She was hurting and broken—and so was he.

"Sounds like Ted's a good guy," he mumbled as he lowered his hands to his lap.

"He is."

Shit, those two little words reawakened the monster. Big. With green eyes. Hell, it was the stuff of her nightmares. And his too, when he thought about it long and hard. The idea of Lily with another man would leave him screaming with rage in his sleep. If he ever bothered to close his eyes long enough to dream . . .

"But he failed the 'keep me safe from the dark' test when he didn't think to camp outside in his car," she added.

"Sometimes all those fancy teaching degrees don't translate to real-life applications."

"No." She cocked her head. "You're not laughing at me. Or telling me there's nothing to be afraid of."

"I told you. I believe you." He reached out his left hand and clasped her right, the one still resting in her lap after holding her dress down to tease him—or just plain drive him crazy. "And, Lil, don't ever let anyone tell you what you should or shouldn't fear."

He gave her hand a squeeze. Then he released her and pushed to his feet. "I'm going back to my post in the car."

"Dominic—"

"Thanks for the coffee." He lifted the mug off the table and held it up in the air as if toasting her. "I'm going to grab a refill on the way out. That way you don't need to worry about the dark tonight. I'm going to watch over you. And after two cups of this brew, nothing will get past me. I promise."

"YOU RUINED EVERYTHING!"

The voice echoed in her ears. The hot breath touched her neck.

Someone screamed. The high-pitched sound reverberated against the walls.

Walls?

She was outside, her body pressed up against pavement. He was on top of her. Breathing . . . touching . . . cutting . . . screaming . . .

No, she was screaming.

But someone had spoken. And she knew that voice. She'd heard it before. Somewhere. Outside of her nightmares. A room filled with desks . . .

No, that was her classroom. She was outside.

Bang. Bang. Bang!

The knocking pulled her back. She wasn't outside. But this couldn't be her classroom.

Her hand reached out. The surface was soft. Familiar. She opened her eyes.

My bedroom.

Another nightmare.

"Lily?"

She pushed herself into an upright position on her queen bed. She'd kept the wallpaper, her old dresser, but she'd upgraded from her twin mattress and metal frame after her mother passed away. Not that it mattered now. She slept alone. And half the time, she closed her eyes and returned to that familiar stretch of pavement in the park.

"Coming." Her voice sounded hoarse. She stumbled toward the bedroom door and made her way down the hall. She paused in the entryway and glanced down at her dress. She'd fallen asleep in her clothes again. It was as if pajamas offered a one-way ticket to an attack she couldn't escape. But in her clothes, she could run.

"Lily, I need you to open the door now or I'm breaking it down," her ex-boyfriend turned bodyguard growled.

She released the chain and flipped the deadbolt. Then she opened the door a crack. "You're up early."

"I never went to sleep." He turned his head as if trying to peer into her house and scan for bad guys. "I thought I heard a scream."

"Oh?" Her grip tightened on the door. "It must have been your sleep-deprived imagination. I didn't . . . I didn't hear it."

He studied her and for a second she wondered if he could see into her thoughts.

"My mistake," he said. "Thought maybe you were calling me in for a morning cup of coffee."

"I was sound asleep."

His brow furrowed. "Did you—"

"I slept great. Thanks for asking," she said before he uttered the word "nightmare." "But I haven't started the coffee yet. Give me ten minutes and I'll invite you in."

She slammed the door and turned the bolt. Then she closed her eyes and rested her forehead against the painted white door.

"Take your time, Lil," he murmured from the other side. "I'll be right here."

She stepped back and headed down the hallway. In her room, she stripped off her dress and tossed it aside. She pulled out the top dresser drawer and rummaged through until she found a pair of flannel pajamas.

Two minutes later, she returned to the front door, turned the lock, and held it open. "On second thought," she said, "I'll let you brew your own."

"Thanks." He walked into the entryway and paused, scanning her up and down. "Cold last night?"

She looked down at the fabric covered with dancing penguins and polar bears. "No. But I love the pattern."

He nodded as if storing that fact for another day, maybe another life when he'd need to pick out a gift for her . . . and settle on clothes covered in arctic animals.

"What time do you need to be at Big Buck's?" he asked as he headed for her kitchen.

"Not until eight tonight. Noah's covering the first shift at the bar." She followed him and opened the fridge as he reached for the coffeepot. "I'm mostly helping out when it gets busy."

"I called my dad last night." He poured the grounds into the reusable filter. And she pulled a carton of orange juice from the middle shelf. The actions felt ordinary and comfortable.

Almost as if I wake up screaming every day and he rushes in for breakfast. After spending the night in his car. . .

"And how is our police chief?" she asked as she poured the juice.

"Fine."

Out of the corner of her eye, she saw him press the start button.

"My dad offered to make us breakfast," he continued. "While he cooks, I can take a look at the file from your attack."

She set the carton and glass down on the counter. "I thought they closed the case."

"Not exactly. The case is still open. They don't have any leads, but my dad agreed that a fresh set of eyes might help." He turned and opened the cabinet containing the mugs with his left hand. "Plus, my father makes a mean omelet."

"I remember."

He glanced over his shoulder. "Honey, if you remembered his eggs you'd be racing to change out of your penguins and polar bears. My father's a damn good policeman. But his omelets are out of this world. Go change. Shower if you want. I'll make myself at home on your couch and wait."

"Do you expect to find something in the file?" she asked. "Do you think your dad missed something?"

"I doubt it." He turned back to the counter and filled his mug. "But it's a place to start. Plus, I'd like to get cleaned up. Maybe while you chat with my dad."

He wouldn't leave her alone. Not even for a shower . . .

And he wanted to find the man. When everyone else said to move on, focus on healing . . .

"You're going to try to find him," she said. "The guy from the park."

He nodded.

He'd promised before. And she'd chalked the claims up to alpha-male bravado. But if he'd asked to see the files . . .

She crossed the room and stopped in front of him, close enough to wrap her arms around him. But she didn't touch him. She rose up on her tiptoes until her mouth was level with his ear. Then she leaned as close as she dared.

"Thank you." She pressed her lips to his bearded cheek. Nothing else touched. One hand on his chest and she might be tempted to show off her red panties again.

Before her lips could savor the feel of his soft beard against her lips, she drew back and met his intense gaze. "And you're welcome to my shower," she added.

"While you're in it?"

She laughed. "I don't think that's a good idea."

"Probably not." He raised his mug to his lips. "But I've spent the last few months hiding from the world in my apartment. Bad ideas are my specialty these days."

She stepped back as if the mounting tension had physical barriers. If she crossed over the line, she wouldn't be safe. She paused by the door. If she went too far . . .

"You'll wait here while I shower?"

He nodded. "You can close your eyes when you wash your hair. Trust me, I'll keep you safe."

She turned and headed down the hall for her bedroom. Out of all the men in the world, why did the one who believed her have to be the same man who'd break her heart when he left again?

Chapter Seven

DOMINIC GLANCED AT the police file that was riding shotgun in his rental. He'd crashed at his childhood home while Lily tended bar. After his nap, he'd slipped out of his dad's farmhouse with the file tucked under his arm. Then he'd picked her up at the bar and returned to his post outside her house. If he took another look now, he might find something he'd missed when he'd scanned the pages this morning over his dad's omelets. Plus, he'd been distracted earlier. Lily's hope had practically filled the fourth place at the kitchen table.

She's counting on me to find something. To put her mind at ease and help her move on. I can't let her down.

He picked up the folder and scanned the pages. But even as he read over the words again, he knew the clue he needed wasn't there. He closed the file and tossed it aside. His dad might be right. This guy could be in another state by now or in Portland, waiting to slash his next victim. Or locked up in a psych ward.

But he trusted Lily's gut feeling. She'd been the one on the ground, the person under attack. And yeah, he'd been there before. He knew that sometimes instinct trumped logic. Plus, this was Lily. She wouldn't lie for attention. She wouldn't make this up.

And he'd promised her that he'd find the guy. If that proved impossible, hell, he'd be stuck here in Forever searching for a damn ghost.

He turned his right hand over, flexing the damaged muscles and nerves. *Stay here* . . . It felt as if he was abandoning any hope of finding his way back to the life he'd had with the army. The finality of that thought—that he was broken beyond repair—sank down like a lead weight pinning him to the seat of the car.

His hand would never work right again. He'd known that when he'd walked out of physical therapy that last time. He wasn't hoping for a miracle.

What's next?

The question echoed in his mind. It had been there for months, but he still didn't have a clue.

He let his right hand rest on his thigh and lifted his gaze to the house lit up like a jack-o'-lantern on Halloween. He'd never pictured coming home to her if things didn't work out with the rangers. Shit, he'd never thought about getting hit, living through it, and getting sidelined. He'd daydreamed about moving Lily and her mom to Georgia even though he knew Mrs. Greene wouldn't leave behind the doctors at the town university. And yeah, he'd hoped Lily would come to him, marry him, after her mother passed away.

But that fantasy felt fucking selfish. He'd lived through that particular loss and wouldn't wish it on anyone. And yeah, there was also a part of him that pictured leaving the rangers at the top of his game. Maybe take a promotion and transfer to the West Coast. If they both lived on the same side of the country, and he didn't spend so much time deployed, then they could make it work. He could provide for her, take care of her.

But coming home to Lily like this?

No, she was part of his reason for leaving Forever and trying to become more . . . better . . . a hero. He'd wanted to come back to her with something to show for his time away following his dream to be the best damn soldier he could be.

And dammit, he'd thought she'd be safe here until then. He'd thought—

A scream pierced through the still night, louder and more forceful than the one he'd heard early that morning. The sound seemingly echoed around the cul-de-sac. But he knew its origin.

He pushed open the car door and headed for the brightly lit house. He didn't have a key, but he wasn't going through the front door. The cries had originated from the bedroom window facing the street—Lily's window.

Bushes lined the side of the single-story home. He stepped onto them, crushing the branches. Yeah, she'd have to replant the flowers, but he needed to reach her. He raised his fist and pounded on the window beside her bed. Inside, he could see her thrashing about on her bed. She wasn't wearing her penguin pajamas tonight. But she'd managed to twist the sheets around her limbs.

"Wake up, Lily!"

He hit the glass with the side of his fist. Pain shot through his hand. But he could write a freaking book about ignoring the sharp pangs at this point.

"Come on," he growled. If she didn't wake up soon, if she kept screaming, he would need to run around the side of the house and slip in through the sliding glass door. But before he tried to break into her home—and possibly throw a rock through the window if he couldn't get through the door—he needed to keep trying to wake her up. He'd shatter her slim sense of security if he showed her just how easy it was to get into her home.

"Lily!" he screamed. "Lily! Honey, open the damn window!"

A wild-haired blonde appeared in the glass. Her blue eyes were wide and so damn haunted his heart cracked.

No, Lily. Don't look at me like that.

Then the pesky organ hardened again. She needed help. Right now, it didn't matter if the threat was out there somewhere, waiting for the perfect time to strike. She needed him *now*.

"Lily, you're OK," he called through the single-paned glass. Thank you, God, that she hadn't replaced the windows. "Let me in. Please, honey."

"No . . . I . . ."

The word drifted through the window, pieces of sentences she'd mumbled to him or someone else.

"It's Dominic," he said. "Please let me in."

She nodded at the sound of his name as if it had snapped her out of the nightmare that held such a tight grip on her.

What had this bastard done to her?

Hell, he'd never wanted to kill. He'd done it, sure. It was part of his job. He'd placed bullets in the hearts of men who disagreed with everything he believed. And yes, on one occasion a woman who'd joined their cause. He'd acted out of duty.

Tonight he wanted to hunt down and hurt the person who'd done this to his Lily. He didn't give a damn that he shouldn't have a claim to her. On some level, she would always be *his*—his first love, his dream . . .

"Lily!"

The window cracked open and he breathed a sigh of relief. A second later, she'd hauled it up and pushed the screen down on his head. He tossed it aside. He'd pull it free from her remaining flower bushes in the morning.

"What are you doing out there?" she asked.

"Waiting for you to open the damn door," he said. "Go around to the front and let me in."

"You'll be there?" she asked. Her brow furrowed and he could read the doubt layered into her expression.

He'd take a swift kick to the gut over that look in her blue eyes. If she couldn't believe he'd be there after she surfaced from nightmare hell . . . shit, he had stayed away too long. He'd pushed too hard against a future with her.

And yeah, he'd made the wrong choices. He should have tried harder to stay in Oregon. He should have said to hell with his military career.

But "should haves" wouldn't rescue the girl rooted to her childhood bedroom. The fear held her captive. He was here now and he needed to save her.

"Yeah, honey, I'll be there. I'd climb through the window, but I'm not sure I'll fit." He hadn't played football in years, but he still had the build of a linebacker.

She nodded and backed away from the window. When she reached the door to her room, she broke into a run.

He climbed out of the destroyed bushes, ran across her front yard, and reached the front entrance as she flipped the deadbolt. He heard the familiar click and then the door opened.

I'm not waiting for an invitation.

Two steps and he stood inside gathering her into his arms. "I've got you, Lily."

He kicked the door closed behind him. And he kept his good hand pressed against her lower back. The muscles in his arm contacted, unwilling to give an inch. His free hand ran down her long hair, smoothing it away from her cheek as she turned her head and rested the other side against his chest. Her hands moved around his waist. And her palms remained flat as she ran them up his back. She reached his shoulder blades and paused, her nails digging into him.

"Nightmare?" he murmured.

She nodded. And hell, the movement sent shockwaves

through his body. He wanted to feel her against his bare skin, her lips on his chest. Her mouth pressed to his . . .

But he couldn't. Not now.

"It's the same one every night," she whispered.

"Ah hell."

He scooped her up, slipping his right arm under her legs, and carried her to the couch. He sat and cradled her on his lap, her bare legs draped over his thighs. She drew them up as if trying to curl into a tight ball on top of him. The long-sleeve shirt she'd worn to tend bar earlier rode up, revealing a hint of black lace panties. He lifted his gaze to her face. She could be bare-ass naked and he wouldn't touch her.

She doesn't need deep kisses and roaming hands tonight.

Her head leaned back against his arm and her face turned up to his. "I need you to catch him," she murmured. "As long as I know he's out there, I can't sleep. I close my eyes and he's right there with me, cutting me and telling me it's all my fault."

"It's not," he said firmly. "Honey, you're the victim. You did nothing wrong."

He raised his right hand, the one he'd been floating in what felt like midair since they'd settled onto the couch. He knew better than to rest it on her legs. She was all bare skin and curves. But he hadn't known where to place it.

Until now. He cupped her cheek and ran his thumb up to the edge of her lips.

She captured his hand and drew it away.

"Lily, I wasn't trying to—"

"You're a victim too," she cut in. "Of war. You're scarred too."

"Yeah."

She interlaced her fingers with his. "How do you sleep at night? How do you escape the nightmares?"

"I don't sleep much anymore," he admitted. "But I don't have nightmares."

He couldn't get comfortable. With his injuries, with the new life those bullets had set in motion . . .

"I just can't," he added.

She nodded, still holding tight to his hand. "What if we took turns? I'll watch over you. And you can watch over me."

Dammit, he didn't need a babysitter while he slept. He wasn't worried about the bogeyman lurking behind closed doors. And if someone busted in? He could take them out with his bare hands. He didn't need a gun or a change in status to "currently enlisted." He had years of training to put to the test if necessary.

But Lily didn't take without offering something in return. Plus, she'd spent so long caring for others—her mother, her father, her students—the offer was probably second nature.

"Sounds like a plan," he said.

"Good." She shifted off his lap and onto the couch beside him. Her long legs reached for the opposite arm as she pulled the throw blanket draped over the back of the sofa down onto her. The grey covering stole away his view, but then she rested her head against his thigh and he was grateful for the blanket.

He would have survived the next few hours staring at

her lace panties and all of the tempting skin her underwear and T-shirt failed to cover. But there was a part of him that wanted to keep her awake, that wanted to take their little game of "I'll show you mine if you show me yours" from the other night to the next, very naked level. That part of him was pretty damn close to her face right now, and hard to miss.

She lifted her right hand and captured his. She intertwined their fingers. Then she drew their joined hands down to rest in front of her body.

"So you don't slip away while I'm sleeping," she said.

"I'll be right here as long as you need me. I promise."

"I know." Her eyelids drifted shut as if the exhaustion was finally taking hold, thrusting aside her near-constant worry. "You never once left without saying goodbye. It's not your style."

But I always left.

He stared down at the messy pile of blond hair strewn over his legs. He studied the fading red reminder of the attack on her cheek. He was hard-pressed now to see why he'd left.

The army. Your duty. Your drive to serve. . .

Yes, that was a part of him even now that he'd been sidelined. But why had he pushed Lily away? After her mother died, he should have come home, gotten down on one knee, and taken her back to Georgia. They could have bought a house near the base.

But I never would have been there.

She would have been alone while he deployed, removed from the hometown that loved her and could comfort her while she grieved. But dammit, he should have given her the choice instead of pushing her away.

He looked up and stared out into the dark night beyond the sliding door. On some level, he knew there was more to his messed-up logic. He'd wanted to be more—a man at the top of his game—before he claimed her.

And I fucking failed.

There would never be anyone else for him. He'd always known that even if he'd tried to bury that truth from himself.

Her hand gave his damaged palm a squeeze and he glanced down at her. Her eyes were still closed. And she finally looked relaxed. Peaceful. And yeah, he'd given that to her. For tonight.

But how the hell did he become the man she needed in her life beyond the sunrise?

Chapter Eight

LILY RAISED HER hand and prepared to give the martini another shake. Maybe, after another round—or ten—she'd also shake off the ridiculous impulse to curl up half-naked on the couch with the man who'd walked out of her life over and over.

Shake. Shake.

The man who'd made it clear he hadn't come home to stay. The man who didn't bother to leave the house unless he had someone to save—

"Easy there," her boss called. Noah stepped in front of her and gently slipped the thoroughly mixed drink from her hand. "I know this is only your second martini, but you just need to shake it for ten or fifteen seconds. If the customer orders it stirred, then you can go to town for a full minute. But if you stir with that much energy, you won't have anything left in the glass."

"Sorry." She handed the chilled glass to Noah.

"Not a problem. I don't expect all the kindergarten teachers that I hire to make a mean martini the first time or two."

He flashed the easy smile he'd worn back in high school and the years afterward. He'd lost it for a while after he'd left the marines. But ever since Josie had walked back into his life, he seemed to be more and more his old self.

She stole a glance at the brooding, bearded man sitting at the far end of the bar. Maybe with enough time and care, Dominic could find his way back too . . .

Except "back" for him was the army. And she wasn't in any position to help him. Not when she still woke up screaming at night.

"Look, I'm not trying to stick my nose where it doesn't belong," Noah said after the waiting customer disappeared with her drink. "But does your desire to shake that drink into submission have something to do with our friend sipping coffee at the end of the bar? I can make Dominic wait in his truck if that would be easier for you. To be honest, I wasn't a hundred percent on board with Josie's plan to drag him back here. Though I do think he needed someone to kick his ass into gear."

But I'm not sure I'm the one for the job. Even though I'd like a glance at his ass. . .

She turned her gaze to Dominic. "No, I asked him to come inside."

Even though part of her still held a grudge for how he'd pushed her away over and over while he went off to save the world, she wanted him here. She craved security and last night he'd provided. Along with eight hard inches of proof that he wanted to do more than peek at her panties . . .

She looked down at the rubber mat beneath her feet. Why did it have to be him? After all this time, why did she still want him? And what was she going to do about it?

"If you want him here, Lily, he can sip coffee all night," Noah said, his voice gentle and so damn kind.

"Thanks." She looked up at the man who'd been by Dominic's side almost as much as she had in high school and for some time afterward. "He's reviewing the police file for me. I was hoping to talk to him about it during my break."

Noah nodded, his expression flashing "Pity! Pity" in the same way the neon Big Buck's sign announced the bar's location to the cars passing by outside. "I'm glad he's being useful for a change."

"He's been a big help so far," she admitted. "He's . . . comforting."

To the point I want to slip into the back room and take a very different type of break.

"Good. Since he was shot, we haven't heard much from him. And before that it was all threats." He raised his voice and looked over her shoulder in Dominic's direction. "I'd rather have him looking out for you than throwing punches at me for knocking up his little sister."

Dominic raised his mug in a mock salute. "Just waiting for the right time."

The door leading to the back room swung open and

Josie walked in with the squirming baby in her arms. "Right time for what?" she demanded.

"To take a swing at him," Dominic said.

Josie marched past the service entrance to the back of the bar and down past the row of empty barstools to where her brother sat. "Well, before you try to fulfill your big-brother duties, I need you to hold Isabelle while I kiss her father."

Dominic accepted the little girl, who looked like she'd rather be set loose to crawl around the barroom floor. But as soon as she settled onto her uncle's lap, she let out a squeal of delight and reached for his beard.

If he hadn't been holding the baby, Lily would have picked up the martini shaker and hurled it at him. Lying with her head on his lap and feeling the proof that he still wanted her had dialed her desire up to a nine. But seeing a glimpse at the future she'd always wanted—Dominic and a baby—pushed her into that dangerous place where she wanted something she couldn't have.

Lily looked away in time to see Josie slip into Noah's arms and kiss him, long and hard, audience be damned.

"I can do a lot of damage with one hand," Dominic called.

Josie broke away from Noah. "Oh, stop it, Dom. If you wanted to hit him that badly, you would have come back and done it a while ago."

"Probably," he acknowledged. The little girl on his lap tugged on his beard and he turned his attention to her.

Having dealt with her brother, Josie turned to her. "How are you?"

And wasn't that a loaded question. *Still terrified of my own shadow* felt like the wrong answer. But *feeling like my ovaries are doing backflips at the sight of your brother with a baby* would probably lead to questions she couldn't answer. From Josie, Noah, and of course the man who managed to leave her feeling pissed off, turned on, and safe, all at once.

"Fine," she said, though she stopped short of forcing a smile. That would probably be overkill.

"Josephine," Dominic barked. "Stop looking at her like that. Lily is not about to fall apart. And if she was, bringing her in to work here probably wasn't your brightest idea."

"I know she's not," Josie snapped. "And there's nothing wrong with working here."

"Noah has a reputation for taking in strays." Lily jumped in before the siblings took their fight to the next level.

"Strays?" Dominic said.

"That's just because Noah picked up a box of kittens," Josie explained.

And hired Josie when she came back to town, then quickly added Caroline to the staff.

Dominic slid off his stool. "Noah, how about giving Lily a break. Between the two of you and the baby, you should be able to manage the Sunday-afternoon crowd."

"Sure." Noah accepted Isabelle, easily lifting the jubilant little girl across the bar. "The back room is all yours. I sent Caroline a text telling her not to come in today. Too slow."

"Thanks." Lily slipped around the happy family. She lifted the piece of polished wood separating the liquor and taps from the patrons. "I'll be back in fifteen. Then you can take off if you'd like. Now that I know how to mix drinks, I should be able to handle things here."

Noah blew a raspberry on his daughter's belly and Lily picked up the pace, dragging her longing with her. Dominic stood by the swinging door to the back room. She rushed toward him as if he could offer the future she'd wanted since high school. And maybe this time, he could give it to her—or a piece of it anyway.

She focused on the police file in his hands. Maybe Dominic had found something his dad had missed. Maybe he could slam the door on the feeling that someone was out there, hunting her, and it would stay closed. *If* he found him.

"Take your time—"

The door swung shut behind her as she followed Dominic into the back room, blocking out Noah's voice.

The Employees Only space held an industrial-sized dishwasher on the right, complete with stainless-steel surfaces for loading and storing the racks. Boxes of liquor, wine cases, and kegs lined the walls. A door stood in the back, leading to the staff parking area. Lockers lined the wall on the left. Another door, this one to a bathroom, stood at one end. And a desk, piled high with papers, filled the remaining space.

"It's more storage than break room," she said.

Dominic nodded and headed for the desk. He set

down the file. Then, he picked up a pen, moved a few things around, and located a notepad.

"Have you found something?" she asked. "In the file?"

"No," he admitted. "But I have an idea."

Her hope surged but was quickly chased by doubt. What if he was trying to calm her? What if he wanted to avoid another night on her couch watching her sleep? He'd refused to let her take a shift watching over him. She'd waited until the sun rose, when her fears subsided, to offer. Still, the answer was no. Instead, he'd driven her over to his dad's place and taken a shower while she'd enjoyed eggs with the police chief again.

"I know you probably did this for one of the deputies, but I want you to make a list of anyone who might have held a grudge against you."

She accepted the pen and paper from his outstretched hands. "You're right. I did this at the station. I couldn't come up with many names though."

"No angry ex-boyfriends?"

She raised an eyebrow. "Aside from you?"

"I'm not upset with you, Lily." He ran his hand through his overgrown locks. "I'm just . . ."

"Determined to show the world your surly side?" She carried the pen and paper to the desk and sat down.

"I'm pissed off at how everything turned out." He folded his arms in front of his chest and leaned back.

"You can't change the past." She glanced down at the blank piece of paper.

"No, but I can do something with your list. More than

my dad and his deputies had time for, I'm guessing," he said. "My father is good at his job. But he has a lot on his plate. When all the facts pointed to a random guy, and no other leads appeared, well, he set the case aside. It's been weeks and there's no proof someone is after you."

Except in my imagination.

"It felt personal," she said. How many times had she repeated those words? Each time hoping that someone would believe her. Because if they couldn't catch him, if they couldn't put an end to her paranoia, how was she going to show up for school and teach her kids? She couldn't tend bar forever. She barely knew how to shake up a drink.

I belong with five-year-olds.

"Is the list I made for the police even in the file?" she asked.

"It is," he said. "But I want you to start from scratch. And take your time."

"This won't take long," she said as she picked up the pen. "My dad is the only person I've argued with recently. And I think I would have noticed if he came after me with a knife. Plus, he's back in rehab. Court-ordered this time after a driving-under-the-influence arrest."

"Did he have any friends? Someone who might pick up his cause?" Dominic demanded.

"I put one of his old drinking buddies on the original list. Your father looked into him and said he was locked up in Salem that day. Plus, the guy who attacked me was younger. The men who spend their days drinking with my father aren't physically fit."

"What about at work?" he asked.

She felt him move behind her and read over her shoulder as she jotted down the names she'd placed on the list for the police. "I get along with all of the other teachers. I love the principal."

"Anyone jealous of Ted?" he asked.

"Again, just you."

She added three additional names, writing "new" in parenthesis next to each one. Then she turned and handed him the paper. "Two disgruntled parents and a guy I met in a bar during a girls' night out. I never learned his last name and I don't recall what he looked like, but he went home with my friends. Shelby might know. She's a librarian in town."

"I'll start with the unhappy parents." He scanned the list. "Want to tell me what pissed Louis Stanton off?"

"Nothing really," she said. "He wasn't listed as an approved adult to pick up his son. I think it had something to do with his divorce. I couldn't let him take his child, but he was very pleasant. He took the form and agreed to send it in to the main office. I'm not sure if he did, but he didn't show up at pickup again. According to his son, he works out of state."

Dominic raised an eyebrow. "A five-year-old would know that?"

"You'd be amazed at what they pick up. On the first day of school last year, one of my kids informed me that her parents always sleep naked."

"Another important fact to know for dismissal time?"

"Not exactly."

He glanced down at the list. "What about this last name?"

She sighed. "Mitch kept trying to send his son to school with a peanut butter sandwich. And we're a nut-free school. He is hotheaded, but not the right build."

"He could have hired someone," Dominic pointed out.

"Over peanut butter?"

"Didn't say it was likely, but it's a place to start." He folded the list and slipped it into his pocket.

"You really are taking this seriously." She stood and came face-to-chest with a wall of muscle covered in a plain black T-shirt. She placed her palms against his chest and looked up at him. "Thank you for believing me."

"You've never lied to me." He covered her left hand with his right. "And it's not like I have a lot going on right now. I've got the time to play detective."

Her free hand moved as if needing to touch more, to feel his skin. She traced the curve of muscle through his shirt. She reached the neckline and traveled over his collarbone to his throat. He'd possessed a powerful body before he'd been shot. And while he'd lost weight during his recovery, he'd clearly spent the months since his release working out. She could feel the power beneath her fingers.

She glanced up. His beard appeared wild. But coupled with the long hair, the facial hair seemingly softened the football star turned soldier.

What would it feel like to kiss him?

His beard had blown past the scratchy phase weeks,

maybe even months, ago. Not that his facial hair stood between a kiss and walking away. She couldn't escape the fact that this man wasn't right for her. As soon as he found her attacker and made sure she was safe, he'd leave again. He always left.

But then what was the harm in kissing him now?

This time, she knew going in that he wasn't permanent. She'd spent so long believing she could have a future with this man. But over the past six years, she'd come to terms with what she needed from a relationship—permanence and trust. If she ever pulled herself together and broke free from this nightmare, she could find a man who could deliver both—and maybe the family she craved. If she found him, she could fall in love again. Right now, she was too broken, living in fear of the dark, her shadow, her own closet . . .

And so was Dominic.

OK, he probably wasn't terrified by the thought of opening the door to his closet to pick out shoes. And if the bogeyman—or the guy from the park—tried anything with him, well, Dominic would likely take him out. She had a feeling he could do it with his bad hand tied behind his back.

Still . . .

After all this time, maybe they were finally in the right place, at the right time in their lives, to be just enough for each other in the present.

"Don't take this the wrong way," she said, keeping her voice low as she ran her hand over his beard and cupped his jaw. "But I'm going to kiss you."

She detected a hint of a smile beneath his beard. "Just so we're clear, what is the wrong way?"

She rose up on her tiptoes and pulled her other hand free from his hold. "This kiss isn't an incentive to do a little detective work."

"You're not trying to bribe me with kisses?"

She ran her fingers through his hair. "I'd start lower if that was my plan. And the um, evidence"—she stole a quick glance at his lower half—"beneath my head last night suggests that you'd agree."

His left hand brushed her chin, tilting it back until her gaze met his. "No, I'd start with your lips. But, honey, I know I make a better bodyguard than a boyfriend for you—"

"I don't need a boyfriend right now. I just need—"

Crash!

Her body tensed and her fingers dug into Dominic as she swallowed the word "you." Fear dominated her senses, stripping away the desire as if her need to kiss the man holding her close was nothing more than a Band-Aid waiting to be ripped off. She heard footsteps, but she couldn't see who had burst in.

Because her "bodyguard" had taken control.

Dominic pulled her close as he guided their bodies back, away from the desk, and through the partially open door leading to the bathroom. "You're all right," he murmured. "You're safe."

She nodded, trying to digest the words. At some point, she'd released her hold on his jaw and pulled her hand free from his hair. Her fingers now clung to his biceps. She needed his strength now, not his kisses.

But I still want that kiss.

She heard voices—plural—in the bar's back room. There were two people out there having what sounded like a very private discussion.

"Caroline." She formed the name with her lips, barely daring to whisper and give away her hiding place.

Dominic nodded. And the second person spoke again.

Josh Summers. The bar's resident baker.

She pulled free from Dominic's hold. One step backward and she felt the sink. She leaned against the vanity's edge. If she hadn't let the fear take over, they would be out there kissing right now. Caroline and Josh would have taken one look at the couple making out by the desk and retreated to someplace more private.

But if she didn't live with fear hovering around her and waiting to strike, if she could snap her fingers and return to her old self, then Dominic wouldn't be here. And if he had returned under different circumstances, she would be looking for a future he couldn't provide.

Dammit, why did Caroline have to choose this moment, when Lily was on the verge of giving in to a feeling that had nothing to do with fear? Why now, when Lily had been ready and willing to steal a kiss from Dominic, did the dishwasher have to burst in and shatter the moment and leave her hiding in the Big Buck's bathroom with the man she wanted to kiss?

Chapter Nine

"SOUNDS LIKE SOMEONE else decided to tackle the bodyguard-versus-boyfriend question," Dominic murmured more to himself than the frozen, wide-eyed woman behind him. His training had kicked in when he heard the door swing open and he'd turned his focus to erasing Lily's rising fear. Now, he moved to the other side of the door, which stood ajar.

But he sure as shit was out of practice, because he'd landed them in a windowless bathroom. And the threat? Noah's pie-throwing friend and Josh Summers, a guy he'd run into a time or two in Forever or around the neighboring town, Independence Falls.

"Why do you bring pies?" Caroline asked, her voice direct and clear.

Was "pie" a code word? Judging from Caroline's guarded expression, and the way Josh followed her into the room as if he wanted to be as close to her as she would allow . . . yeah, "why do you bring pies" must translate into something not suitable for work.

"I like to bake," Josh said. The next few words were lost, but the sentence ended with the word "memory."

Hell, maybe they were talking pie and Dominic had Josh to thank for spending his first night in town wearing marionberries.

"Noah didn't ask you to keep an eye on me?" Caroline demanded. Based on her tone, Josh Summers had better hope she couldn't get her hands one of his pies—or her gun.

But the youngest Summers brother seemed oblivious to the threat. He merely laughed, then said: "Noah doesn't want me anywhere near you. He doesn't think you're ready for a relationship or the things that go with it."

We shouldn't be eavesdropping on this. We should go out there, tell them we're here and ask them to take their pie/sex talk somewhere else.

Dominic glanced at Lily, who was still holding the vanity's edge as if she needed support. The other couple's arrival had clearly triggered her lingering anxiety. If he marched her out there now, her fear would be on display. He couldn't do that to her. But he couldn't leave her here.

"I'm not ready." The words carried the first tinge of fear in Caroline's voice. "If that's why you're still coming around, after all this time . . . you need to move on. I don't know if I'll ever be ready. I haven't had sex because I wanted to in years."

Ah hell, no wonder everyone in Forever believed Noah hired strays. First he'd taken in Josie. And Dominic now knew about the loss she'd suffered even if she'd tried to hide it from everyone. Then, Caroline—

"There's no timeline," Josh said. "After what your commanding officer did to you, I don't expect you to start trusting strange men you meet in the forest overnight. I'd be in trouble if you did. This is timber country. You're bound to come across loggers in these woods."

"There's a big difference between overnight and a year, Josh."

She's military. The pieces fell into place. And he'd be willing to guess, this was the woman his best friend hadn't been able to save. Noah had mentioned that he'd been serving alongside a woman that he hadn't been able to help. Dominic had assumed she'd been hit. Flying shrapnel. IED. Not rape. His best friend had never mentioned rape by a fellow soldier.

"Plus, I'm still hiding," Caroline said.

"No one knows you're here," Josh said firmly. "And we're going to keep it that way."

Fuck. And he thought he had issues. This woman had run from her duty to serve.

"I'm not worried about Duncan finding me and blaming me for ruining his career," Caroline said. "I'm AWOL. I shouldn't be here. I should be serving . . ."

The pie-throwing dishwasher was running from the military. And Dominic knew that unauthorized absences came with serious consequences. If she was caught, she could end up behind bars. Probably a worst-case scenario, but still.

"Caroline."

Dominic had a feeling Josh now stood pretty damn close to her. He stole a glance through the cracked door. And yeah, Josh was within arm's reach of the woman with the long black hair. The dishwasher was petite. Her oversized Big Buck's T-shirt, cargo shorts, and black combat boots didn't help.

"I bring the pies because I like you," Josh said.

And Dominic had bad feeling this moment was about to get a little too intimate for comfort—his and possibly Caroline's as well. In which case, he'd be forced to storm out of the bathroom and tackle a man he hadn't seen in half a dozen years.

"I like the way you fight to keep going," Josh said, his voice just loud enough to reach the bathroom. "That's not easy. I like the way you lick your lips after a bite of pie. And the way you listen to me talk about my brothers and their families."

"There are plenty of women who would listen to you talk while eating homemade baked goods," she challenged. "Are you *sure* Noah didn't ask you to drop by? Look out for me?"

"Noah wants me to stay the hell away from you because he's afraid one day, I'll do this."

Dominic had a pretty good idea what "this" was, but he watched through the crack in the door just in case the man he'd played ball with once or twice growing up tried to take advantage of his close proximity to Caroline.

And yeah, Josh did. But as soon as his lips touched

Caroline's, the heels of her combat boots lifted off the ground. From where Dominic stood it looked like she was deepening the kiss. But then she drew back, her fingers lifted to her lips.

"I've waited over a year for that kiss," Josh said, slipping his hands into his pocket as he moved out of Dominic's line of sight. "I don't care how long I have to wait for the next one. Take all the time you need, Caroline. Your kisses are worth waiting for."

He heard the door slam and knew that Josh had left. But Caroline stood rooted to the floor, staring straight ahead with her fingers still raised to her mouth.

"Caroline?" Dominic could hear Noah's voice, but couldn't see him. "Are you all right?"

Caroline turned and faced the door leading to the bar. "How much did you overhear?"

"Not a damn thing. We have Isabelle out here demanding to practice her crawling skills on the floor."

"Liar," Caroline said.

And Dominic had to bite back a laugh. As far as he knew, Ryan, himself, and now he'd guess Josie, were the only ones who ever called Noah out. His friend had always been the town golden boy, above reproach except to his closest friends.

"It's none of my business either way," Noah said. "You asked me to stay out of it and I have."

"Thank you," she said.

"I also know that if you didn't want him to kiss you, he'd be on the floor howling in pain," Noah added. "Now come on out when you're ready."

Caroline marched forward as if following an order, not a request from her friend and boss. He heard the door swing shut, and finally, they were alone again.

He turned to the woman he'd nearly kissed in that room not long before the interruption. Years ago, she'd given him a kiss that promised to bring him back desperate for another. The memory of that moment in his truck had pushed him to achieve more and more. So that when he came back, he'd have something to offer her. A hero for a husband if she still wanted him. A solid foundation that would allow her to follow her heart's desire after so many years of caring for her mother.

He formed a fist with his right hand. He couldn't give her those things now. But she hadn't asked for a hero. Before they'd been interrupted, she'd demanded a kiss. And he didn't want to wait another year, another month, or another day for that offer to come around again.

"Lily."

She lifted her chin. Her grip had relaxed, but she kept her fingers wrapped around the sink's edge. The position left her chest thrust out and her full breasts pressed against her shirt. Years ago, he'd known how to kiss her, how to touch her, and how to love her. Now, he didn't have a clue. But he suspected one kiss wouldn't be enough.

"You can call me whatever you want. Boyfriend. Bodyguard. I don't care as long as you kiss me. Now. And, honey, I'm not—"

Lily's body fell against his and it no longer mattered that he hadn't added "waiting a year" to the end of his declaration. She'd moved so fast that he hadn't seen her push off from the counter surrounding the sink.

Her hands ran over his chest, up to his shoulders, and down his arms. Her fingers linked with his as her body pressed close. He groaned as she rose to her tiptoes and her breasts brushed his chest.

We should have gotten naked first.

But then her lips pressed against his and he forgot all about T-shirts. Sure, her breasts remained front and center in his mind as she drew closer . . . until her lips parted and her tongue touched his.

Lily.

His body responded as if hopeful she might kiss him lower. But they weren't there yet. Not even close.

He pulled his hands free from hers. He had to touch her. *Now.* His palms glided up her arms, over her long-sleeve T-shirt to her shoulders, and down her back. Her left leg lifted and wrapped around his waist.

Be a gentleman and help her.

He placed a palm under her thigh, guiding it higher and higher. Maybe he couldn't fire a gun. But his damaged hand had no trouble slipping under the seam of her panties. She'd left her thong at home today. And though he was tempted to check and see if her underwear matched her dark red nails, he couldn't tear his lips away from hers.

He wanted to stay right here, lost in her mouth and the familiar feel of her body rocking against him. Let the outside world fade away. To hell with what he should or shouldn't do.

Like coming home to stay.

She moaned against his mouth as his fingers explored the blond curls between her legs. And the last hold on his control slipped away.

Without breaking their kiss, he guided her back until the sink was at her back. Then he lifted her up and pressed her legs wide. She, in turn, released him and rested her hands on the vanity's edge. She was open, ready, and kissing him like she never wanted to let him go. The desire to take her, claim her, make her *his* again threatened to overwhelm.

Not in a fucking bathroom.

Hell, if he took her right here against the sink or with her back to the walls, the sheetrock beneath would probably give out. But he didn't need to take out a wall to end their visit to the bathroom with a bang.

He held her waist with one hand as his right drew small circles over her inner thigh. His fingers slipped back under her panties. With her lips parted, his thumb found the spot that would drive her straight into the kind of bliss that would leave her screaming—

"More!" she cried, pulling back from his kiss.

He ran his thumb back and forth, paying attention to the way her hips rocked against his fingers. He ignored the cramping in his hand. He didn't need all of his fingers for this. He just needed to pay attention. A good orgasm was in the details. If he listened to her response, the soft moans, the familiar words, altered his delivery . . .

"Oh . . . my . . . "

He stole a glance at her face. Lips parted, eyes closed, head thrown back, she looked as if she was lost in pleasure. *And I put her there.* Satisfaction swelled along with another part of his body that would require attention later. After. Right now . . .

Her long ponytail teased the faucet as her back arched and her breasts thrust higher in the air. One of these days, he was going to strip off her long-sleeve top and touch every damn inch of her.

"Now! Now!" she screamed.

His gaze dropped lower as her bottom lifted off the vanity's edge. Her skirt was bunched around her waist, her legs splayed and open to his touch. He felt her tighten around the fingers he'd slipped inside her as the climax took hold.

"Yes," she hissed.

Her bottom rose up as her body rode out the pleasure. And her hips reached higher, her feet pressing into the vanity's door. He ran his thumb over her again.

Bang.

Crash.

In one orgasm-fueled moment, her head hit the mirror hanging over the sink and her feet pushed through the vanity's door. Both came apart under the force of her pleasure. The mirror fell from the wall, hit the edge of the sink, and then crashed to the floor. Out of the corner of his eye, he saw broken glass decorating the toilet seat.

The door to the cabinet below the sink hadn't fared much better. She'd kicked it off its hinges. And yeah, he should probably feel something other than pride that he'd driven her to destruction with a single climax. But . . .

Maybe later when Noah gave him hell for tearing up his bar.

Lily lifted her head and opened her eyes as her hips rested down on the edge of the sink again. He withdrew his fingers and stepped back. His hand had blown past aching to outright pain. And he didn't give a damn.

"Are you all right?" he asked.

"That was an amazing kiss," she murmured.

"Yeah, well, I think they heard it all the way in the bar."

She laughed, her eyes bright and her face relaxed. Looking at her now, her fear felt like a distant memory. He knew it would return. And when it did . . . he'd bury his face between her legs.

As if she'd followed his thought process down the path marked "oral sex" and realized that one orgasm in the break-room bathroom was probably enough, she slid off the sink's edge and drew her skirt down her legs.

"The mirror," she gasped as if she'd just realized the mess they'd made. She looked back at him and laughed. "At least now I know you haven't lost your touch for destructive orgasms."

"That was all you, honey." *And my aching dick can back up that fact.*

Her gaze swept down his front and lingered on the bulge in his cargo shorts. He didn't move or try to adjust himself. She'd felt his hard-on when she'd rested her head in his lap last night, and again while they'd kissed. At this point, an erection felt like part of greeting her.

"We'll get to your turn. But right now, I should get back to work. I don't think Noah meant 'take an hour off and wreck the bathroom' when he offered me a break."

"If Noah gives you trouble, send him back here. He can help me fix that cabinet."

She raised an eyebrow. "And how are you going to account for the damage?"

"I wasn't planning on offering him an explanation."

She laughed as she walked out of the bathroom. The sound faded along with her footsteps. Then the swinging door creaked and she was gone.

He rested his hands on the vanity's edge still warm from her naked skin and stared at the place on the wall where the mirror had hung when they'd first rushed into the room, hoping to hide. The ache in his hand pushed hard against his triumph. He'd asked his damaged hand to do too much and now he was paying for it. But it had been worth it. For a few minutes, he'd given them both a brief reprieve from fear and pain.

But it was just that—a break. Nothing more. If he wanted to help her, if he loved her, he needed to focus on making Lily feel safe. He needed to help her get her life back—one that was rooted here and didn't include a fucked-up former ranger. He needed . . .

"To play bodyguard, not boyfriend."

Chapter Ten

"EVERYTHING OK, LILY?"

Noah tossed out the question as he held up the service side to the bar. The room had filled since she'd left for her "break." After the first week at Big Buck's, she'd learned that the university crowd viewed four to five on Sunday afternoon as Bloody Mary and mimosa time. And they were halfway through that magical hour.

She'd heard that question over and over since the attack. But this time, her friend turned boss wasn't referencing her recent trauma.

"How much did you overhear?" she asked.

"Enough to know I should send Caroline out to take drink orders and have Josie leave through the front with the baby." He glanced at the back door. "Dominic still 'reviewing the case file' back there? Or is it safe to send the dishwasher to her station to keep up with this rush?"

"It's safe. Though she might need to bring a broom. The mirror in the bathroom broke."

"That must be some case file. But I'm glad he's helping you." Noah smiled as he handed her a printed list of drink orders. "I'll tackle the Bloody Marys"—which she didn't have a clue how to mix—"if you handle the mimosas."

She turned and reached for three white-wine glasses.

"Lily."

The first glass slipped through her fingers, but she caught it before it shattered on the floor. Then she turned to her new customer. "Ted. What a surprise."

The man, who'd dumped her before their relationship fully launched into boyfriend/girlfriend territory, claimed a barstool across from her. His long, narrow face offered a concerned expression. She had a feeling he used the same carefully planned look at parent-teacher conferences.

"How are you, Lily?" he asked. "Are you OK?"

She'd received the same question minutes ago. But Ted delivered his with a boatload of pity versus sarcasm. Of course, the man sitting across the bar hadn't heard her scream "Yes! Yes! Yes!" through the walls. She'd caught a few of the customers looking at her with a question in their eyes—what's in the back room? And can I visit?—when she'd first walked out, but not Ted.

"I'm fine," she said. "Can I get you anything?"

Please say no. Please leave and stop raining on my orgasm parade.

Not that one climax constituted a parade. But she had

hope for later tonight, after Dominic searched her home for potential threats . . .

Wow, her idea of foreplay needed work. After they caught this guy, after things returned to normal in her life, then . . . but no, Dominic would be gone again by then.

"A cup of coffee if you have it," Ted said, and she could practically feel the rain clouds moving in. "I might have a beer later. I thought I would stick around and keep you company."

But you broke up with me and my "fears."

"Sure, but I have to keep up with the drink orders." She turned her back to him and reached for mimosa glasses. Ted could wait for his coffee.

"If you're pouring coffee, I'll have a cup too." She glanced over her shoulder and saw Dominic sliding onto the stool beside Ted. He held out his left hand. "Dominic. I don't think we've met before. I've been away for a while and you're new to the area."

"Nice to meet you." Ted gave his hand an awkward shake.

She turned her focus back to pouring not-so-equal parts champagne and orange juice into glasses. After keeping these customers waiting, they deserved a little extra booze.

"Sorry, I'd offer my right hand, but it's not a pretty sight right now," Dominic said.

Her brow furrowed as she added the OJ. She'd seen his hand up close. The skin was damaged from where the bullet had gone through, but she'd been under the impression that he was more concerned with the loss of his fine motor skills.

"I cut it on a broken piece of mirror," Dominic continued.

Her grip tightened on the juice bottle. And she waited for him to add *the mirror our mutual friend over there broke while she came against my hand. . .*

"Hey, Noah," Dominic called. "Do you have a Band-Aid?"

"First-aid kit is in the back by the dishwasher," Noah shot back. A side glance at her boss and fellow bartender for the night told her that Noah was moving fast to pick up her slack.

She turned her attention back to the drink ticket. Three mimosas—check. Two bottles of light beer—

"You know, I'm not sure a Band-Aid will work," Dominic said. "Would you look at how much blood has already seeped through this rag?"

She whirled around in time to see Ted's face pale as he stared at Dominic's right hand, wrapped in a red-stained bar towel.

"Oh God," Ted murmured, swaying on his barstool.

"Dominic," she said. "Don't do that. He can't—"

Ted swayed back on his stool and Dominic extended his right arm to catch him.

"Handle the sight of blood?" Dominic supplied.

"You knew," she said, her eyes widening. Because she'd told him, after her failed date with Ted.

She saw Noah leap over the front of the bar and rush to the unconscious customer in Dominic's arms.

"Let's lay him down and elevate his legs." Noah barked

the orders as he reached for Ted. Then he glanced up at her. "How much has he had to drink?"

"Nothing yet," she said. "And that's not why he fainted."

"It's my fault," Dominic replied. "Good Guy Ted can't take the sight of blood. And I showed him this." He held up his right hand.

Noah glanced up, shook his head, and continued to run his hand over Ted's neckline as if the short-sleeve button-down might be constricting. Dominic reached over and tapped Ted's shoulder.

"Hey, Ted," he called. And the man lying on the floor stirred. As soon as the other patrons realized Ted would survive, they returned to their drinks.

"Damn," Dominic said. "And here I thought I was one down with one to go."

Noah glanced at him as he drew Ted into an upright position. "Planning to make another customer faint tonight?"

"Nah." He removed the rag and revealed a cut-free hand. "I borrowed some ketchup from your supplies in the back. Probably left over from when your dad served food in this place."

"Yeah," Noah said. "Why the hell did you pretend it was blood?"

Dominic shrugged and his broad shoulders brushed the tips of his long hair. "I saw Ted when I poked my head out and thought I could get a jump start on the list of guys I'm supposed to knock off for Lily. That's why you brought me back here, right?"

"That was Josie's idea," Noah said, cradling a semi-alert Ted to his side.

"You didn't think to ask Lily first?" Dominic said.

Noah glanced up at her. "Sorry, Lil. Josie thought it would help."

"And what? She has you by the balls? You can't make your own call?" Dominic demanded.

Noah raised his eyebrows. "You want to talk about your little sister's relationship with my balls?"

"I don't think that conversation would end well," Dominic said as Ted started to open his eyes.

"Maybe if you'd come back sooner," Noah said, "you'd be use to the idea by now."

"Doubt that." Dominic stood. "I'm going to finish cleaning up in the back and leave Sleeping Beauty in your capable hands." He turned to her. "Your friend Ted could probably use a glass of fruit juice. The sugar will help when he comes to."

She nodded.

"Let me know if you need anything else, Lily."

"Thank you," she called after him. But he was already walking away. "I'll give you a proper thank you later," she added, reaching for a pint glass and the orange juice.

"Not in my bar you won't," Noah said as he drew Ted up and guided him into a chair. "I don't think this place could sustain the damage."

Chapter Eleven

"I KNOW WHAT you're doing," Lily said as she raised her mug to her lips.

Fresh coffee first thing in the morning was one of the perks of having a caffeine junkie awake on the couch all night. But after living for two days with the memory of the way he'd touched her, she'd debated taking the coffeepot hostage in an attempt to catch him asleep. Then she could join him on the couch and wake him with a kiss that might lead to more. More kissing. More touching.

He'd always touched her with an intensity that bordered on rough. He made demands of her body as if he'd mapped out his moves beforehand. But at some point, his control would slip. It wouldn't make room for hers. Instead, the fierce need to reach the climax would overtake them—and take out everything that stood in the way.

She smiled as she lowered the mug. Maybe they'd even manage to break the furniture.

"What?" he called down.

"I said I know what you're doing."

Dominic raised his hand to block the morning sun as he gazed down at her from the top of the ladder. "Installing floodlights behind your house?"

"You're trying to earn a superspecial oral surprise."

He set the bulb on the top rung and started down the ladder.

"Or maybe sex in your new favorite position. Something wild and kinky you learned while you were away," she continued.

He reached the bottom rung and stepped down, turning to face her. "I must have been deployed the day the rangers offered the 'kinky' sex class."

She raised her mug to her lips, but didn't drink. Instead, she ran her tongue over the rim and waited for his gaze to head south. One . . . two . . . three . . . And his green eyes honed in on her mouth.

If she closed the space between them and pressed up against him, she'd bet that she would receive a long, hard welcome. And it would have nothing to do with her floodlights.

But then he would turn around and walk away mumbling something about bad ideas and bodyguards.

Leaving me wet and ready for sex is a bad idea! It was right up there on her list of Horrible Ideas, next to not coming home after he'd healed, after he'd promised . . .

She'd wanted to hurl the words at him, one after the other. But she also knew he was right. He would leave again. And while she might see that as a reason to fool around without risk, maybe touching her in the Big Buck's bathroom was all he could take. Or his warped sense of duty was getting in the way again. He'd given his all to the army and now he'd do the same to his position as her bodyguard.

Regardless of his reason for keeping his distance, her desire had reached a fever pitch twenty-four hours after the encounter in the Big Buck's bathroom. But Dominic seemed determined to focus on her safety. He'd sent her off to bed when they got back from the bar each night, promising to keep watch while he followed up on leads. She didn't want to distract him from finding the guy who'd attacked her in the park. But her desire to get into his pants, to explore what was once upon a time very familiar territory tore holes in her need for an answer.

She already felt safe and secure. She had him. Maybe not for long, but that was part of the reason it would be so simple to get naked with him. She could strip off her long-sleeve shirts without worrying about her injuries. He had them too. And they could determine whether the coffee table could hold them . . .

"I'm putting in the floodlights so that you can see out into the yard at night. You'll sleep better with them on," he said. "But why don't you go ahead and tell me more about this 'superspecial oral surprise.'"

"It might be better if I showed you."

"I don't know." He shook his head and crossed his arms in front of his chest. "A few days ago, you threw a wine glass at me. I'm not sure I'm ready to let your teeth near a part of my body I would rather keep intact."

"You're holding a grudge because I didn't welcome you with open arms?" Before he'd opened his mouth, she'd been tempted to run her tongue over his forearm, tracing the powerful muscles. Now, she wanted to sink her teeth into him. Which proved his point, but still, he'd promised to return home to her.

"No." He shook his head. "I expected you to kick me out of the bar and call Noah. I got on the plane telling myself I would come out, see that you were all right, then hop the next flight back to Georgia once I knew you were safe."

"But you didn't expect to find me this messed up?" she said, wishing they could return to the topic of BJs.

"Someone hurt you." Fury flashed in his eyes, offering a glimpse of the former warrior hiding behind the beard and long hair. "You have every right to be messed up. Hell, I'm screwed up too." He held up his hand. "I've been hiding in my apartment refusing to face the world. So if there is a prize for most fucked up, I'm betting I win. At least you're out there, trying to put your life back together."

"And you thought you'd find me barricaded in my house? That's not an option for me. I need to go back to my job in a couple of weeks. The one that involves a roomful of kids *under* twenty-one."

"I knew you wouldn't hide," he said.

"Then what kept you from taking that return flight?" she demanded.

"Honestly?"

"Don't you dare lie to me," she said.

His expression softened. "I didn't expect to take one look at you and *want* you so damn much." He stepped forward and cupped her jaw. His thumb brushed over the visible reminder of her attack. "And I'm not talking about my desire to keep you safe."

"No?" she murmured. He'd use the words "want" and "desire." What she felt when he touched her bore a stronger resemblance to take-me-against-the-wall lust. Desire could be controlled. But she'd snapped her restraint in the Big Buck's bathroom. The pieces had probably been swept up with the broken mirror and discarded.

He released her chin and ran his hand down her back. Then he gave a little pull, drawing her body up against his. "I look at you," he murmured, "and I remember every position, every way I made you come, how you felt against my mouth. Honey, I know it all by heart. I don't want to try some new kinky position. I want to revisit where we've been."

Impossible.

After all these years, after all that had happened, she couldn't go back to the uncertainty. She refused to wait for him again. Her life was too splintered now. She required long-term. She needed permanence, stability, and trust.

But right now? With her body pressed against the hard muscles that promised protection and pleasure? Safety coupled with seduction from a man she trusted not to hurt her . . .

Well, he might walk away with her heart again. But if he did, that was on her this time. She understood the risks. And she knew when he said "I'm leaving," he meant it.

But she was willing to take a chance to win a brief reprieve from her constant anxiety.

"I think we've reached a compromise." She lifted her fingers to his lips. "If you don't trust my mouth on you"— she placed her other hand over the hard ridge beneath his cargo shorts—"I guess we know who goes first. But don't forget, you had your chance and you tossed it away."

Dominic captured her hand and held her fingers to his mouth. His lips parted and his tongue ran over the tip of her index finger. Anticipation raced from her hand down to her toes.

"You're sure about this?" he murmured.

"It's part of the bodyguard job," she said before he could remind her that he made a better protector than boyfriend.

He scooped her into his arms and turned to the sliding glass door. "Just remember you asked for this."

"I have a long list of fears," she murmured as he lowered her feet to the ground. "Orgasms don't make the cut."

She stripped off her drawstring shorts and pale pink underwear. Naked from the waist down, she sat on the edge of the coffee table.

"Here?" he asked as he lowered down to his knees.

She nodded, her gaze fixed on the man kneeling in her

living room. His self-imposed uniform only told half the story. Beneath his black cargo shorts and the grey T-shirt that read "ARMY" across the chest, he still possessed the powerhouse body she'd watched on the football field years ago.

But her high school love had always appeared in control. The bearded warrior kneeling at her feet looked as if he'd parted ways with restraint. His hair fell past his chin. And his green eyes held a hint of wicked promise.

"Spread your legs, honey."

And let me show you how much I love you.

The words floated in on a memory from a time when she'd loved the hero, the high school star determined to join the army, to serve . . . But she quickly pushed it away. Falling in love with that man again? Impossible. He didn't exist. He'd been replaced with the hardened man who seemed to hold his fear close to the heart, just like she did.

But she still lay back and allowed her knees to drift apart.

His hands ran up her inner thighs and she closed her eyes. When his fingers reached their destination, his thumbs stroked down her center, and then spread her further. She waited for his lips to brush over her.

"Dominic?" she said softly.

His hands pressed against her legs in response. But if he didn't lick her soon . . .

"It's been a long time, Lily. Let me look."

"Dominic," she growled as she wiggled her hips. It

had been a long time for her too. And her body hummed with need. Looking wasn't going to cut it. She needed his hands, his mouth.

He let out a low laugh. "Impatient?"

But he didn't wait for her response. His hand wrapped around her waist and he pulled her bottom off the table's edge.

"What?" she exclaimed as he cupped one cheek in each hand. Then he lowered his mouth, his large body bent over her as if preparing to worship . . . and then he did. He ran his tongue over her, back and forth.

She let everything go. She didn't need to cry out for him to move a little higher, or dip lower at just . . . the right . . . moment. He remembered. She relaxed into the pleasure, completely at his mercy. His fingers teased her backside, offering a thrill that rocketed forward as his tongue pressed against her, then drew back.

"You still like that," he murmured.

"I like everything," she whispered, trying to rock her hips. But he held her steady, maintaining control of every touch, every taste . . .

"Do you like this?" he asked.

His tongue lifted and was briefly replaced with a brush of his beard, tickling her folds. She squirmed, but he held her bottom tight.

"Oh . . . my . . ." she moaned.

Then his tongue swept over her, moving back and forth with quick, firm stokes. Her body rose to the edge, and he drew back. His beard brushed over her increasingly sensitive skin. One swift pass over her and then fast strokes reminiscent of a vibrator returned.

"Dominic!"

The pleasure peaked as if it had been waiting for her to call his name. And he continued to lick and stroke, holding her tight, offering another gentle press of his fingers to draw out the . . .

"Oh," she groaned as the pitch-perfect feeling faded.

He released her and she lay with her lower body hanging off the edge of her coffee table and her upper half melting into the wood.

"You did it wrong," she murmured. "The table is still in one piece."

He laughed. Then she heard movement and sat up, sliding off the coffee table and onto the floor. He looked ready to push off the ground. She reached out, clasping his wrist. "Where are you going? It's your turn."

He glanced over her shoulder. "What time did my sister need you at the bar for inventory?"

"Ten."

He nodded to her mother's old clock hung on the living room's far wall. "It's nine forty-five. You slept in while I was setting up your lights."

"Slept in?"

"That's what happens when you start sleeping again. You can't stop. Or so I've heard. You'd better get dressed now. I'll drop you off on my way to breakfast. And I'll have my dad cook you up something so you don't go hungry."

She turned and flashed a wide grin. "That was my breakfast. It was called 'Oh . . . My . . . Dominic.'"

He shook his head. "Breakfast of champions."

"Don't worry," she called as she raced to her room. "You'll get yours after my shift."

It wasn't until she'd returned to the front door fully dressed that she realized what she'd done. She'd opened her closet without worrying what might jump out at her. For the first time in six weeks, she felt safe and happy.

And the man responsible was sipping a to-go cup of coffee while he stared at her coffee table.

"Trying to figure out how we're going to break it tonight?" she asked.

He nodded as if she'd asked him about the position of her new outdoor lights. "I have a few ideas."

Chapter Twelve

DOMINIC WALKED UP the porch steps he'd built along-side his father back in high school. They'd gone from one project to the next after his mother died. His mom had made list after list of plans, things they could tackle later, when his father wasn't so busy at the station. And they'd done them all. After he graduated, Dominic had tried to involve Josie, mostly to keep an eye on her while she was grounded.

He paused on the top step and stared out into the yard. They'd started with a vegetable garden, and then moved on to larger construction projects, him and his dad both trying to stave off the heartache and loss.

After spending another long night on Lily's couch fighting the urge to climb into her bed, then getting up at dawn to install a camera on her front porch and flood-lights in her yard, he needed a shower and a nap. Lily was with Josie for now, completing the inventory at the bar. But Dominic had promised he'd be at Big Buck's in time to help her set up. Josie and Noah had a meeting at a brewery up by Portland, and Caroline wasn't due in until close to five o'clock. Not much need for a dishwasher on a quiet weekday afternoon.

But he could smell the fried eggs and bacon from here. And his dad's cooking still trumped sleep in his book. Dominic pushed open the door. His father stood by the stove, an apron covering his police uniform as a line of fried eggs sizzled on the skillet. Three placemats sat on the four-top in the kitchen.

"Where's Lily?" his dad asked.

"Work." He sank into a chair as his father plated breakfast.

"I thought she'd be with you or I would have called with the news." His dad deposited one plate in front of him. "But it might be better for you to hear it first."

"News about what?" Dominic plucked a piece of toast off the plate in the center of the table.

"The Salem police called yesterday and reported a similar crime. Young woman attacked while jogging."

His hand froze, still holding the bread over his plate. "Attacked with a knife?"

His father nodded. "He spoke with one of my deputies. I wanted more details before I told you and Lily. When I called him back, the chief said they had a suspect in custody and they'd like Lily to come up."

"He's tall and broad shouldered?" Dominic had read

through the case file so many times he knew the description by heart. "Wearing a sweatshirt?"

"No sweatshirt this time, but the suspect wore a mask."

Dominic nodded. He'd reviewed the case file and come up with next to nothing aside from a belligerent dad who picked fights over PB&J and one locked in a custody battle. But none of that involved Lily.

He stared down at his plate, his teeth grinding together. He knew damn well that she honest to God believed she'd been the target of the attack, that there was a reason a knife-wielding lunatic had come after *her*. But he also knew how hard it was to swallow the fact that sometimes you were just in the wrong place at the wrong time—like in front of a terrorist with a gun.

He'd wanted to support Lily. And yeah, he wanted a chance to crush the guy who'd attacked her. So he'd tried to replace the facts with new ones. He'd allowed his feelings for Lily to cloud his judgment.

"He took the victim's phone," his father added between bites of egg. "The Salem PD used it to track him."

Dominic buttered his toast, his brow furrowed. "That doesn't fit. The guy who attacked Lily never went for her cell. She was listening to music on it. She had it in her hand when those girls found her. He never tried to take it."

His father set down his fork. "The man they arrested isn't a hardened criminal. They found prescription antipsychotics on him. Enough to suggest he hadn't been taking his meds."

"Are you sure they were his?"

His dad nodded. "They ran his prints. He's been arrested before. Mostly public disturbance, that sort of thing. And a long psych record."

"Did he confess to attacking Lily?" he asked.

"No." His father let out a sigh. "The suspect claims he's never been to Forever. Never heard of it. And they didn't recover a knife. Just the phone."

"How many times was the Salem victim slashed?"

"Just a few. Mostly on her arms and face. No deep cuts. I have a copy of the report at the station. I can bring it home for you this evening and you can share it with Lily. The Salem victim's name has been blacked out, but she can get a sense and decide if she wants to drive over and try to ID the guy. The mug shot's in there too."

Dominic nodded. "I'll come back for it. And she'll want to go to the station and talk to the Salem PD. She'll need to hear the details. She's convinced that she knew her attacker. And hell, I was too. But knowing he's behind bars will help her sleep at night."

"You too, I imagine." His father picked up his fork, but kept his grey-green eyes focused on him. "Still keeping watch from her couch?"

"For now."

"Does this mean you're heading back to Georgia?" his father asked. "Now that there's been an arrest?"

"I don't know." He stabbed the yolk and watched it run over his plate. Then he picked up his toast and dipped it in the gooey center. His dad cooked the perfect egg. It might be worth staying just for that. "I still have the apartment out there. And I'm not sure what I'd do with myself here. It's not like this area has a lot of jobs right now," he added.

"I've been waiting for you to ask me for a position. I didn't want to push. But with your military experience—"

"I still can't fire a gun," Dominic cut in.

"Have you been out to the range? Tried your other hand?"

Yeah, he had. Back in Georgia, before he'd given up hope. But he was a shitty shot with his left. He could do it, sure. But hit a target? Defend a teammate? Not a chance. Being able to pull a trigger didn't make a man a ranger or even a policeman.

"Dad, I'm not the best man for the job. There are plenty of guys, probably some fresh out of the military, who still have the full use of both hands."

"What about a desk job?"

"It's my right hand. My handwriting wasn't anything special before, but now I'm struggling to sign my own name." He stabbed his eggs. "I've thought about it. Trust me, I tried to see if there was something I could do for my guys, my team. A support position. I'd push paper around an office at the base if I thought I'd be useful." He shook his head. "They have guys with prosthetics who can do a better job."

Playing bodyguard, watching over Lily, that job fit him. But beyond that he saw himself back in Georgia, trying to give Lily the space she needed to find the man who could complete the life she wanted. If he stayed here, he'd be tempted to make her next boyfriend faint off his barstool—or worse, he might try for the position himself.

"You might find more people willing to help you here." His father wiped his mouth and pushed back from the table. "Now that Josie's moved into her own place with Noah and the baby, I wouldn't mind having you here."

"Thanks, Dad." But he didn't want his hometown's pity heaped on him day after day as everyone else moved on with their lives—including Lily.

THE SMELL HIT her as Dominic walked into the bar. He closed the door and turned the lock, keeping the public securely on the other side until Big Buck's opened for business at noon.

"You picked up Chinese? At eleven something in the morning? I think this not-sleeping thing is messing up your internal clock." She ran a cloth over the bar's polished wooden surface.

She'd completed the inventory with Josie and together they'd set up for her shift. Noah had arrived minutes before Dominic to drive Josie up to their appointment at the brewery. Her friends' and coworkers' movements were carefully orchestrated to keep her feeling safe.

Until Dominic took a detour for Chinese, leaving her alone for five minutes. Still, she'd survived. And that was something, wasn't it? Progress?

"I thought we'd celebrate," he said.

Dread rippled through her. He was leaving. The army had found a job for him. Or—

"The Salem police have a suspect in custody," he said.

She dropped the cloth. "What?"

"There was another attack," he explained. "Only this time they were able to make an arrest."

"And they are sure it's him?"

He nodded as he set the take-out bag on one of the high-tops. "The physical description matches. Same body type. And the attacks were . . . similar."

There was another woman out there who'd been cut over and over for no reason. Another person who would spend months asking why? And coming up empty, eventually forced to accept the fact there wasn't an answer.

"He wasn't after me." She drew her arms tight around her waist. She'd been so sure. Now, it felt as if the one piece of the nightmare that she'd clung to had been torn away. Her memory felt faulty, and her judgment questionable. How could she have been so wrong?

"No. He wasn't," he said. "And you're safe now."

But she wasn't. Couldn't he see that? If she couldn't trust in her own judgment? Her memory of her attacker's words?

"You can go up to the Salem police station and talk to them in the morning," he added.

She'd dreamed about this. Not when she drifted off to sleep, but in the moments when she'd stared out into her brightly lit home, listening for suspect sounds. She'd envisioned how it would feel to know that man she feared was behind bars. But where was the relief?

"Are you sure?" she asked slowly. "I don't want to know what your dad thinks, or the Salem police believe. Do *you* think they have the man who attacked *me*?"

"I read what the Salem police chief sent over. So,

yeah, I think it is a strong possibility. And once you read through it . . . I think you'll finally be able to sleep at night."

"I slept fine last night."

"Because I was on your couch," he said.

And I don't want you to abandon your post.

She nodded slowly. "I thought if I knew who'd attacked me, I would feel . . ."

"Liberated?" He walked around the bar, lifted the service entrance, and stepped into her domain. "Like your life can finally return to normal?"

"Yes."

He pulled her into his arms. "Sounds like someone forgot to program your on-off switch."

Resting her chin against his chest, she looked up at him. "Is that your way of saying I should give it time?"

"Everything won't go back to the way it was overnight," he said.

"Will you stay?" she asked, promising herself this was the last time she'd say those words to him. She wouldn't beg him to come back. And she wouldn't wait for him. Not this time. But she might crumble if he left her now. Every little sound would leave her terrified. And how could she comfort herself, allow logic to explain away the supposedly spooky sounds as harmless—leaves rustling in the trees—when she'd been wrong before?

He nodded. "For as long as you need me."

She rose up on her tiptoes and her heels lifted out of her sensible slip-on shoes. She pressed her lips to his cheek. One soft touch, before she drew back. "That could be a long, long time."

He brushed her hair back from her face. "You won't need me to watch over you forever," he said.

How can you know that?

"You're going to heal," he continued. "This is only the beginning. Once you see the file and talk to the police, the truth will sink in. Trust me."

She nodded. Maybe he was right. "But I need you to stay until then."

"I will. I promise I will stay on your couch for as long as you need me."

And then he would slip away again. Without a sense of purpose to keep him here, he'd return to Georgia. Taking the pleasure he'd delivered on her coffee table with him . . .

But not before she returned the favor. Pushing aside her fear and her questions about her own judgment, she let her fingers drift lower, down over his T-shirt.

"I don't want you to take this the wrong way," she said as her hands moved between them, searching for his waistline, her fingers eager to release the button on his shorts. She found her target and undid the closure. Hooking her thumbs into his underwear, she dragged his clothes down to the floor

"But," she began as the rubber mat dug into her knees. Thankfully, she'd selected a pair of capri-length legging in her dash to get dressed. Because she planned to stay here awhile. He'd changed his facial hair, added a few scars, but the hard, long length ready and waiting for her remained the same.

"You're going to ask me to trust you too?" he said as his hand ran through her hair.

She pressed her lips to the tip. She felt the moisture beaded there.

And the door leading to the back room swung open.

Her nails crawled at his thighs. But Dominic had already jumped into action, pulling up his shorts. He didn't bother to secure the fly as he hauled her off the floor and held her close against him.

"Hey, guys," Josh Summers called. "Drop something back there?"

"You could say that," Dominic said, still holding Lily close, as if concerned her fears had taken flight. But the nervous questions—who was there? Why was he here?—had slipped away. Just Josh and his bad timing.

But maybe he didn't see it that way. One glance around Dominic, and she saw Josh's amused smile.

"Glad to see you made it here, man," Josh said. "Josie called and asked if I'd bring Caroline over just in case you were delayed. Help Lily open the bar and all."

And babysit her, she thought.

"According to the sign outside," Josh continued, "this place opens in five. You might want to search the floor later."

"Noted." Dominic released her and fixed his pants.

Josh rocked back and forth on his boots, his smile still firmly in place. "Or you could give the college kid peering in the window, hoping for a beer after class, one helluva view."

"Shouldn't you be helping the dishwasher?" Dominic shot back.

"Consider this my good deed of the day," Josh said, his smile broadening. "Though I'm guessing you might feel differently right about now."

"Josh," Dominic growled.

"Before you threaten to 'shut me up' or something," Josh said, "remember I have three older brothers. I can take anything you throw at me. Plus, I slept last night. You look like you haven't had a solid eight hours in weeks."

Try months.

Josh Summers had a point. She patted Dominic's chest. "Go home, Dominic, and get some sleep," she said. "You're going to need it. Because you're not staying on the couch tonight." She leaned up and added in a whisper: "And we won't be sleeping either."

She felt the tension ripple through his body. And behind them Josh Summers laughed.

"Lily," Dominic murmured, looking down at her. He placed his hand over hers. "I'm staying either way. You don't have to—"

"I know. I want to." She pressed her lips to scar on the back of his right hand, still resting on top of hers, covering his heart. Her lips still touching his skin, she added, "I want you."

Even though I know you'll leave again.

Chapter Thirteen

I'M AN IDIOT.

Dominic accelerated, pushing the rental car past fifty,
fifty-five, sixty . . . He hit sixty-five and held steady. He
was willing to risk a speeding ticket. Hell, he knew most
of the guys on the force. They'd probably let him off with
a warning. But he wasn't going to crash the car because
he'd gone and fallen asleep at his dad's place.

An hour or two, he told himself, just until Noah returned to the bar and took over for Lily. But he'd gone
and slept past sunset. It was eight o'clock. Lily had been
home for hours, probably wondering where he'd gone, if
he'd left . . .

No, she had to know he'd say goodbye. He wouldn't
slip away in the middle of her shift. And he would never
leave her afraid.

He stole a glance at the file folder riding shotgun. It
held the Salem arrest report and mug shot of the guy

who'd attacked the woman in Salem. A detailed report they could review in the morning, after he calmed her down. She had to be terrified by now, alone in her house, after dark.

"Fuck. Fuck. Fuck." He slapped his palm against the steering wheel as he turned onto her cul-de-sac. Everything was calm, quiet. Lights shone through the windows of the neighboring houses, but Lily's looked as if she wished to illuminate the whole damn block.

He docked his car in front of her house, the right front wheel riding up onto the curb. Hell, he'd fix it later. Tomorrow. He opened the door and sprinted up the steps. He raised his fist and pounded on the door. And . . . nothing.

"Lily!" he called. "Come to the front, honey."

He stood under the front porch lights, the side of his fist still resting on the door. He could walk the perimeter of the house, peering in the windows. He had a feeling he'd find her huddled in a corner, trapped by her own damn fears. She needed him. In there. With her. Holding her. Loving her . . .

He stepped back and examined the door. Then he called one more time, "Lily!"

Nothing.

He eyed the keyhole. The door opened in. It wouldn't take much. Just a well-placed kick. He raised his right leg and aimed his boot. The door gave a little, but the deadbolt refused to break apart and grant him access. He kicked again.

"Dominic?" He heard her voice on the other side, followed by footsteps.

"I'm right here, Lily," he called back.

The locks turned. The chain released. And she pulled open the door.

"What are you doing?" she asked. Her eyes were wide. He studied her face, searching for signs of the terror he'd witnessed after her nightmare. But she wasn't pale-faced and ready to fling herself into his arms. Her long hair spiraled down over her shoulders. The ringlets teased the top of her white bath towel.

Her right hand rested on the door and her left held the towel's closure, nestled between her breasts. The faded scars, the healed wounds from where he'd sliced her forearms, stared back at him. Dozens of small cuts intended for her beautiful face. His anger welled. And he wanted to tear apart the man sitting in a Salem jail cell. How could anyone hurt her? His Lily? So beautiful, so sweet . . .

"Dominic?"

He lifted his gaze and met her blue eyes. "I'm sorry. You didn't answer. I thought you might"—*need me*—"be waiting for me somewhere in the back." *Afraid.*

"I was getting ready."

He stole a glance at her toes. Bright pink polish caught the light. Knowing that she'd painted her nails for him . . . yeah, his need to get inside had nothing to do with worrying if she was having a panic attack.

"For you," she added, drawing his attention up her towel-clad body to her mouth. A smile teased her lips. "But thank you."

"For trying to break into your house?"

"For coming back to me."

"I'm not running away from you." He moved closer and raised his arm. He placed his hand above hers on the door.

"Not tonight you aren't." She stepped back and tugged on the top of the white towel, pulling it free. It fell, forming a pool at her feet. "Would you like to come in, Dominic?"

Desire roared through him. But he held on to the damn door. When he let it go, when he unleashed his need to take her, claim her, make her *his* again, hell, he hoped this house could take it.

He let himself look at her, really look, now before he pulled her close. He remembered her soft curves, the feel of her skin. The four-inch line on her right side—that was new. And while it was healing like the others, it had cut deeper.

He moved on, taking in the swell of her hips, the blond curls he'd explored earlier, her thighs—

"Dominic?" she asked softly as she shifted her weight and raised her arms, crossing them in front of her naked chest. "I know I'm not the same—"

"I love how every inch of you looks and I always have." He walked in, slamming the door behind him. He placed his hands on her hips and kept moving, backing her up against the wall. The archway leading to the living room stood to his left. The couch. The coffee table. But he couldn't wait. He wanted her here. Now.

He ran his hand down over her hips. "I'm crazy about your curves. Always have been."

His palms glided over her ass to her thighs. He lifted

her up and her limbs obeyed, wrapping around him like they belonged right there clinging to him. He pressed her back against the bare surface, pinning her there as he slipped one hand down and withdrew the condom he'd slipped into his pocket earlier. He tore the packet open with his teeth. Then he reached down between them, freed his aching dick from his shorts, and covered himself.

"I love you just like this." He ran his thumb over her clit, down lower. One swift stroke. And then he thrust into her. He gave her a second to adjust. But he couldn't wait. Her legs tightened around him and he began to thrust.

"Just." He pressed deeper. "Like." He withdrew an inch and then another. "This." And he flexed his hips. "Lily."

HE CAME BACK.

Lily squeezed her thighs and dug her heels into the back of his shorts, still covering his ass. Her hand clawed at his T-shirt. If she'd known, if she'd suspected they'd end up here, she would have demanded that he strip on the porch. She didn't care if the neighbors saw. They probably already hated her for leaving the floodlights on.

But she'd started to wonder if he'd left already. It was only a matter of time . . .

He thrust harder, faster, and the wall at her back trembled. She tried to focus on the slide of his cock, the feel of his hands holding her legs as if it was nothing. Head back, eyes closed, she tried to hold tight to the moment.

But his desire roared like a beast that had burst in determined to awaken her own need.

"Do me a favor," he growled. "Hold your breasts."

He drew back and watched as she raised her hands to her chest and cupped the bouncing flesh. Her palms brushed her nipples as he pressed his cock home.

If only he considered this home, the place he belonged...

"That's it," he murmured as he reached between them.

His other hand still supported her bottom. And his body pinned her to the wall, rocking back and forth, but never leaving her room to fall. She heard a wine bottle tumble off the rack that shared this stretch of wall in the living room.

"We're making a mess," she whispered.

"Honey, in a second you won't give a damn," he promised. His fingers found her clit, rubbing back and forth. "I can't hold out much longer. It's been ... too ... long."

He groaned as he pushed harder, taking more from her, sinking deeper.

"Oh wow." Her fingers pressed into her breasts. The sensations—from her chest, to the thumb dancing over her clit, to his cock pulsing inside her—spiraled together, pushing her closer. "Oh, Dominic!"

Her head thumped against the wall and she let go, trusting him to hold her, to keep her safe, while she drifted away into a place where pleasure dominated. Each moment tried to surpass the last, offering more, more, more ...

And then she felt the descent take hold, drawing her

back to the panting man holding her against the wall. She opened her eyes and met his gaze.

"I'm going to let you down," he said. "But don't for a second think that I'm done with you."

He gently lowered her legs and stepped back. And she obeyed. She remained rooted to the floor, her back leaning against the wall. "I need you to . . ." she began, panting through words.

"Anything," he said as he disposed of the condom.

"I need you to take off your clothes."

He raised an eyebrow. "Fair is fair and all that?"

She shook her head from side to side as he reached back and pulled off his T-shirt. "I love your curves too. The shape of your biceps, the way your waistline tapers down. The lines of your muscles disappearing beneath your pants."

"Careful, you'll make me blush."

"Turn around and let me admire your backside," she said. He obeyed, planting his feet hip-width apart and letting her look her fill. Her gaze touched on the place where a bullet had slipped out after nicking one of his major arteries. But she didn't linger there. As far as she was concerned, the proof that he'd risked his life for his country only added to the perfection of his muscular back. And his ass . . . she could stare at his butt forever.

"Looked your fill?" he asked without moving one perfect muscle.

"Are you blushing yet?" she teased.

"Yeah, but I know a good place to hide my face until I recover."

He turned around and walked over to her. Then he sank to his knees. She gasped as his hand touched the back of her thigh, her nerves still clinging to her last orgasm, unwilling to part with the pleasure just yet.

"Lift your leg, Lily. Rest it on my shoulder."

"Dominic—"

"Shh." His lips brushed the place he had teased earlier as his hands explored her backside. "It's my turn to make your cheeks turn pink."

WRAPPED AGAIN IN her towel, Lily sank down onto the couch, holding a glass of red wine from the bottle they'd knocked to the floor earlier. Her partner in orgasms and destruction had retrieved his boxer briefs but left the rest of his clothes in the hallway. While she'd opened the wine, he'd grabbed the cocktail shaker she'd sent flying off the top shelf of the bar when he'd tried his best to make her blush, and mixed a drink.

"No coffee tonight?" she asked.

"No. I caught enough sleep earlier to skip the caffeine for a few hours." He raised the martini to his lips.

"May I have a sip?" she asked and he obliged. One taste was enough to confirm her suspicions. "You make a much better martini. The customers at Big Buck's would love this. And I bet you know how to pour a beer and change a keg."

"Trying to talk me into a job at Noah's?" he asked mildly. "I thought he'd already taken in his share of strays."

"With the baby, I'm sure he could use another bartender." She ran her finger over the rim of her wine glass and tried not to build a fantasy future in her head. "I'm only filling in. But even when she's in town April is only part-time."

"He could always train my sister to bartend. She's been waiting tables there long enough."

She shook her head. "Josie wants to focus on her assistant manager role when she's not with Isabelle."

"Lily, are you trying to talk me into a job working for my sister?"

"Just while you're in town," she said. "I know you're still planning to go back."

He nodded.

"Why?" she blurted out.

She'd held this question back since he had first walked into the bar. She'd asked others. Would he stay? Why had he come back? But she'd been too afraid to hear the answer to this one. When he'd first come home, she'd told herself that she'd moved on—with Ted. But even before Mr. Good Guy had handed her flowers and an apology, she'd known she was lying to herself. She didn't love Ted and she probably never would, not the way she'd once loved the man sipping a martini on her couch.

So she needed to summon her courage. "If there someone waiting for you? Back in Georgia? After I walked away, after you got out of hospital—"

"No." His eyes widened. "After what we just did? In your hall? And you think . . . Jesus, Lily. No, there's no one waiting for me."

But she kept going, spelling out her fears that had nothing to do with dark corners. "After I left, did you fall in love with someone else? Is that why you didn't come back even after you'd healed? After you received an honorable discharged. Did you finally find someone worth staying for?"

"I swear there's no one else, Lily. There never was." He let out a low, bitter bark of laughter as he raised his good hand to his hair. "I tried once. I picked up a woman in a bar a few months ago. But I couldn't . . . she wasn't you."

"One woman in all those years?" she asked, allowing her disbelief to slip into her tone. "All those deployments?"

She'd remained faithful to him. Even when he broke up with her after Ranger School, claiming the long distance wouldn't work due to his deployments and her mother's constant need for care. But she'd always wondered if he'd taken advantage of their time apart. But to wait until after he'd sent her away for the last time? After he'd been discharged and her mother had succumbed to her illness?

"One," he said. "All it took was a single kiss and I sent her home."

"You never slept with anyone else?"

"Only you."

She wanted to believe him. But she'd felt his hunger for pleasure. Tonight, against the entryway wall, he'd made love to her as if his desire ruled him, not the other way around. How could he have pushed all that need aside for so long, not knowing if they would ever find a way to make it work?

The stark truth stared back at her. They'd only made love a handful of times in the past five years. And he'd never turned to anyone else?

"Only me," she said. "For all those years? All the ups and downs?"

His green eyes narrowed. "If you don't believe me, why did you make love to me?"

"That wasn't—"

"Why did you let me fuck you in the hall?" he demanded. "Why did you get down on your knees in the bar earlier? Why, Lily?"

She stared at the hard lines of his face. Even now, his frustration and anger rising up, the answer was clear. "Because I'm safe with you. I can stop looking over my shoulder. I can feel something other than fear when I'm with you. I can escape with you for a little while."

"Until I leave and head back to Georgia?" he asked.

She nodded.

DOMINIC STARED AT the woman he'd loved since he was in high school. He could still smell her, and taste her. Even the feel of her clit lingered on his tongue. He'd explored the most intimate parts of her.

But he was nothing more than a stopgap. He was comfortable, like a teddy bear. Familiar. Safe. And heading out of town as soon as her life went back to normal. She didn't have to worry about falling for him all over again, or awakening dormant feelings.

And he didn't either.

Because he still loved her.

Back in Georgia, holed up in his room with his feet on a damn box, he could pretend he'd loved her in another lifetime. But his heart had always belonged to her. He'd spent most of his life trying to be a better man for her. He'd wanted to give her a future she could trust. She'd grown up with an alcoholic who'd spent more time bouncing from rehab to drunk than he ever spent at a job. Dominic had wanted to give her the best of himself.

And he'd found that with the army. Then it had been blown away. Maybe he could find it again. He hadn't yet. But it was time to start looking.

"Have you changed your mind?" she asked. "Are you thinking about staying? Asking Noah for that job?"

Hell, maybe it was the alcohol or the fact that he'd finally gotten some sleep. Or maybe his mind was playing tricks on him, but he swore she sounded hopeful. And he wanted to say yes.

But barely six weeks had passed since her attack. And now that they'd caught the guy, her fear would start to fade. Or what if it didn't? What if her fear held tight and he stayed, never knowing if she loved him or simply wanted a security guard who made her come so hard the walls and tables shook?

"We need to make sure they have the right guy first," he said. "Then I'll decide."

She nodded. "Did you bring the arrest details?"

"They're in the car." He set his martini on the coffee table. He'd lost his taste for it now. "I'll go get the file."

"No, let it wait until morning," she said. She set her

wine glass on the table and stood. With one hand on her towel, she extended the other. "Come to bed with me."

"I slept most of the day," he said, ignoring her outstretched hand. "I'll be fine on the couch. I can keep watch tonight. Make you feel safe."

Fulfill my role as your bodyguard and try to remember I'm not your boyfriend anymore.

"You can keep watch while you hold me," she said. "Please. Lying in your arms—that's the safest place in the world."

What the hell could he say to that? He wanted to be her sanctuary, the person she ran to when she needed help. But he wanted to be so much more.

Maybe Lily saw the truth. He wasn't ready to love her the way she deserved to be loved. She should have a man in her life that could give the best version of himself to her—in bed and out. Dominic could fuck her against a wall and watch her back. Beyond that?

Hell, he didn't have clue what the best version of himself was anymore.

But he stood and followed her down the hall. He checked behind the door and scanned the bathroom for her before she went in to brush her teeth. Then, he stripped off his boxer briefs as she dropped her towel, and climbed into bed with her.

She rolled onto her side, facing the window. The curtains were drawn tonight, he noted as he moved behind her. He wrapped his right arm around her and pulled her back until her backside pressed up against his dick.

And while the rest of him couldn't hide from the fact that he'd bared his heart and soul tonight and she'd challenged him, unable to believe he'd never wanted anyone else, his dick rose to attention at the contact. But he ignored his physical response to having the woman he loved in his arms. Because not once had she said the words he needed to hear.

"Dominic?"

"Yeah?" His lips brushed her bare shoulder.

"There was never anyone else for me either," she whispered.

Those words. I needed to hear you say those words.

"I tried with Ted," she continued.

His muscles contracted, drawing her closer to him, as if trying to pull her away from the past and Ted, who sure as shit didn't have any business being in bed with them.

"But there was never anyone else. Not while you were in training or deployed. It wasn't until you had the chance to come home and didn't . . ."

"I wasn't ready." He pressed his lips to her shoulder. Hell, he still didn't know if he was.

"I know," she said. "But, Dominic, I can't wait anymore. I want to have a family and build a future. So if you decide to stay, if you tell me you will, I . . . I need you to mean it."

"I won't lie to you." He ran his hand down her body, caressing her curves and drawing her back. "If nothing else, you can trust me."

She reached up, wrapping her arms around her neck.

Her body stretched out before him, granting him access. Her legs parted and he slipped his hand between them, touching and stroking.

"I know I can," she said dreamily as her hips rose up to his touch. "I think you were the only person who believed me when I was convinced the man who attacked me knew me and wanted to strike again."

His hand stilled. Shit, he'd already lied to her. Earlier, when she'd asked him if they had the right guy, he'd said yes. But he knew there were inconsistencies. Still, he'd let her believe she was safe. In the end, she would know when she saw the file waiting in his car. She'd be able to judge for herself. She was the only one who could make that call.

"Dominic?" she asked.

Damn, he'd messed this up. He'd let his need drive him. He'd nearly kicked down her door tonight. And he hadn't been hell-bent on handing over the file. He'd wanted to sink into her, claim her, fuck her.

God, he was an ass.

"You don't have to stop touching me," she said, still looking up at him as if he was a good guy. "I have a box of condoms in my nightstand."

"You do?" And yeah, that pulled his attention away from the fact that he wasn't anywhere close to a perfect score when it came to being the guy for her. "How old are they?"

"They're new. I bought them in case—"

He cut her off with a kiss. Her lips parted beneath his,

granting him access and kissing him back. Slowly, once he felt he'd proven his point—they weren't going to say Ted's name again while lying naked together—he drew back and reached for the nightstand.

He reached into the drawer and pulled out papers, a book, and finally the sealed box of condoms. He ripped it open and tore off a packet. He was tempted to use every damn one in the box tonight. So she never got the chance to with Ted or anyone else.

"I know what you're thinking," she murmured as he covered himself and turned to her. "You want to use them all tonight."

He leaned his head back and laughed. "Lily, I'm just a man. Six condoms in one night?"

"Hmmm, I see your point," she murmured as he settled between her legs.

He wanted to take this slow, ease into it and draw out every stroke. He wanted to make her come again and again even if he couldn't manage a six-condom night. Hell, seven if they counted the one from earlier.

Gently, he pressed into her, allowing her time to adjust. He tried to hold back the last few inches, but her hips rocked up to greet him. Her legs wrapped around him, her heels digging into his ass. And she began to move.

Fuck slow.

He drove into her over and over, rushing toward the finish line. Next time, they would try for gentle and calm. Right now, he wanted her too much.

"Dominic," she said as her arms drew him down until his chest pressed against hers. And her lips brushed his ear. "We can make balloon animals with the rest of them. There won't be any left after tonight."

He heard the implied *for anyone else* in her words and came with a rush as she followed him, tumbling into pleasure.

After . . . still trying to breathe . . . he rolled off her and stared up at the ceiling. What if he tried to be a part of Lily's life—the man who delivered her dreams of marriage and family—and failed?

He reached for the box, determined to use another in ten minutes. Maybe eight if she kept rubbing up against his side.

"Again," she whispered.

"Again, Lily."

Just in case they had the right man in custody. Just in case her life went back to normal and she didn't need him anymore. Just in case he was left with a choice. Stay with the woman who owned his heart, knowing she no longer needed what he had to give her—protection—or go. And he decided to leave again.

He wanted to make damn sure that box wasn't waiting for Ted or anyone else.

Chapter Fourteen

LILY SURVEYED HER bed. The pinks sheets had been tucked in and the comforter folded on the edge while she'd been in the shower. She'd heard him out here, moving around. And she'd closed her eyes while shampooing her hair, knowing he was right there.

"Everything all right?" Dominic walked in and handed her a cup of coffee. Her childhood bedroom felt smaller with him standing beside the queen-sized bed that barely fit. Though it hadn't seemed that way last night.

She accepted the coffee. "We didn't break the bed."

"Pick up another box of condoms and we'll try again after our trip to Salem."

The attack. The man sitting in a jail cell. The report from the second attack . . . She'd let it all slip to the back of her mind for one blissful night. "Do you have that file? The one from the Salem police department? I'd like to look at it before we go."

"I brought it in from the car." He turned and led the way down the hall. When they reached the kitchen, he set down his mug and picked up a thin manila folder off the counter, then handed it to her.

Her fingers trembled and she glanced up at him. "Have you read it?"

He nodded. "There are some differences," he said slowly. "And without your positive ID they don't have anything to tie him to your attack. He claims he's never been to Forever."

Unease washed over her. He'd sounded so sure yesterday, in the bar. "But he used a knife?"

"Yes. And the woman was out jogging. But this time he took her phone."

Lily closed her eyes and the memory rushed in. Lying on the pavement . . . crawling . . . hoping . . . screaming . . . and then finding her phone.

She opened her eyes. "Mine fell, I think." Goodness, she couldn't even say for sure. And now it mattered. "Maybe he didn't see it."

"Maybe," he agreed and he cocked his head. "Do you want to sit down? Then look?"

"No." She flipped open the folder and scanned the page. " 'Give me your phone'—those were his only words?"

The pieces didn't line up. Her body felt as if it had been turned to stone. Dominic had been so sure, but this crime was different. The suspect used a knife, but only after the victim refused to meet his demands. The man who attacked her in the park had cut first.

She looked down at the mug shot. She didn't need

to read anymore. It didn't matter if she'd dropped her cell phone or how many times she'd been cut versus the woman in Salem. The man sitting in a jail cell was irrelevant.

She looked up at Dominic. "It's not him. I saw his eyes. This isn't him. This man has bright blue eyes. The man who attacked me had brown ones. A deep, dark brown."

"You're sure?" he said.

"Yes." She closed the file and set it on the counter. Then she looked up at him. "How could you be certain it was?"

"The pieces lined up. Another random attack . . . It seemed plausible. I wasn't certain, but—"

"I've believed from the beginning that the man who came at me with a knife was after *me*. I never thought it was random. I know what your father and the rest of the police force thought, but . . ." She studied his resigned expression. He almost looked as if he'd been waiting for this. "Did you ever believe me? You told me that you did. But all this time, you agreed with your dad and . . . and everyone else."

"No." His tone was strong, forceful. "No, Lil—"

"Do you believe me now? Do you think someone is after *me*?" she asked. "Or you think I'm just plain afraid?"

He ran his hands through his long hair. "I believed you. But I also know myself. I wanted the guy who hurt you to be out there, waiting for me to take him out. I wanted to crush him."

She nodded as the truth sank in. Looking back, he'd always wanted to play the part of the hero, even if it meant fighting somewhere far away, living on the other side of the country—even if it kept them apart. And she'd always let him. She'd always believed in him.

"And I let all that bullshit cloud my judgment," he said. "Look at the facts. There were no links to anyone in your life. You never received a death threat. And no one has come after you. I know you're afraid. That's normal after what happened to you. And shit, Lil, I wanted to help you. I still do."

"Did you really look into the names I gave you?" She needed to pinpoint when he'd dismissed the idea that someone wanted to hurt her.

"Yeah, I did. While you've been at the bar, I've slipped away to my dad's and used his computer. I've combed through every reference to those names online and in the police databases. There was nothing to find, Lil. I would have told you if there was. I came home to help you, honey."

"Ryan dragged you back here." She felt her faith crumbling. She'd placed so much trust in Dominic, and for so long. Even when he'd left Forever six years ago to become a soldier.

But that had been taken from him. And now . . .

"My fears aren't some project for you practice playing the hero again," she added.

"Is that what you think I've been doing here?" He raised his right hand. The scar was visible from across the room. "I'm no hero. Hell, I'm not even cut out for the bodyguard role Ryan, Noah, and Josie dumped on me.

I'm here because I love you. Do you hear me, Lily? I love you."

"No," she whispered. His words hung in the air, tossed out if he'd needed a trump card. Something to steal her attention away from the truth right in front of her. But how many times had he said those words only to walk away from her?

"You needed someone to help you through this. And yeah, I'm the wrong guy for the job because I care about you too damn much. Because I want you too damn much."

I love you too.

She closed her eyes. It was real. She knew it in her heart. But she couldn't tell him that. Not now, as the hard truth of her situation sank in. He'd come back because he loved her and she'd been hurt. But if she hadn't needed someone watching over her night and day, he would have stayed away. He would have continued loving her from freaking Georgia.

If that was his idea of love . . . she didn't want it. The kind of love couldn't give her what she needed. She'd known from the beginning that the sense of security he offered felt tenuous at best.

"You're right," she said, opening her eyes. "You're not a hero. You're a coward. So go. Leave. You were planning to anyway."

"Lily, I'm not leaving you like this."

"Fine, then stay." Whether he chose to remain in Forever or go back to Georgia didn't matter. And it never had. How she felt in his arms, safe and secure, or whether he loved her or she loved him, none of that mattered if she couldn't trust him. Because what she needed from him, what she needed for herself—that required trust.

"But if you stay," she added, "I need you to leave me alone."

"Lily—"

"I can't fight my way back from this if you're out there, watching my house from your car." Her voice trembled with every word, but she pushed forward. She needed to say these words out loud and make sure he understood.

And let him know that she did too, because he wasn't the only coward in the room. She'd been burying her head in the sand when it came to facing the awful truth of her situation.

"If I need you, or a police officer, or anyone, watching over me, checking behind every door in my home before I can enter a room, I'll never feel safe again," she said, her voice gaining strength with each word. "I can't wait for someone to show up and hand me back my sense of security. I need to find it on my own."

DOMINIC HAD BEEN shot three times, but he had still wanted to climb out of his hospital bed and fight the minute he woke up. It had taken him a long time to accept defeat. But right now, he recognized failure. He'd had it all wrong from the beginning. He should have tried to be her boyfriend, not her protector.

But hell, even then he probably would have failed.

"You're right," he said. "I'll go."

Because if he stayed . . .

He could make her feel secure, he could work to win her trust back, and hell, he might even be able to give her the family she craved one day. But he would never be able to witness Lily's fear or see her in pain and not do whatever he could to keep her safe.

He loved her too damn much.

And he loved her because she was willing to push him out of her life and find her own way forward. He loved her because she took what life handed her and faced it head-on. When her mother was sick, and later when she was dying, Lily had stayed by her. She could have left her mom, married him, and lived with him in Georgia. But Lily never turned away when life dealt her a rough blow. He might have gone to war, but she was right. Compared to her, he was a coward, hiding for all those months in his Georgia apartment.

"I'll go and I won't camp out in front of your house." He tried for a smile, but it felt a helluva lot more like a grimace. "You have your floodlights now. Plus, I managed to install that camera on your front porch."

"Thank you," she said. "That will help."

He walked toward her and she stepped aside, allowing space for him to slip past. He paused. "I'll take the file back and let my dad know that we jumped to the wrong conclusion."

She handed over the manila folder. "He'll keep the case open?"

"Yes. And, Lil, you have to promise that you'll call him or call the station if someone threatens you. If you're right, and he's out there . . ."

She nodded. "I will."

He reached out and ran his good hand over her cheek. "I'll see you around."

"You're not going back to Georgia?"

"No." He made the decision in a split second. And not because she needed him here. This was his home. He couldn't run from that fact any longer. He still didn't have a clue what the future held, but he'd face that sad fact here.

"There's nothing for me in Georgia," he continued. "It's time to call it quits on my extended pity party." He withdrew his hand from her face. "When does school start again?"

"Staff returns in two weeks. I'll have some time to set up my classroom before the kids arrive."

He held back the words "you'll be OK by then." He couldn't know for sure and he was done lying to her—or telling half-truths. It didn't matter if they ran into each other in the grocery store and she asked how he was doing. He wouldn't lie. If he were heartsick over her new boyfriend, he'd damn well tell her.

"Take care, Lily."

He turned and walked out of the kitchen. He headed straight for his blue rental, his limbs moving on autopilot while his heart begged and pleaded with him to turn the fuck around. He ignored that pesky organ. The damn thing had survived two rounds to the chest. It would live through this latest heartbreak.

He turned on the car, and at ten in the morning, drove to the one bar in Forever that he knew would let him in. And Noah damn well better serve him.

Ignoring the Closed sign, he pounded on the door. Five harsh knocks and his fist met with air as the door swung open. His best friend, the high school quarterback Dominic had busted his ass to protect on the field, stared back at him.

"Mistaking this place for a coffee house now?" Noah asked.

"I know you have a pot made. I can smell it from here." Dominic pushed past him and walked into the empty bar. He claimed one of the barstools. "But right now I need to chase it with a shot of whiskey."

Noah closed the door and walked around behind the bar. He poured the coffee. Then grabbed a bottle from the top shelf. It looked fancy. But hell if Dominic cared right now. He wanted it to burn going down and knock some sense into him.

"Is that all?" Noah asked dryly.

"No." Dominic tossed back the shot and slammed the glass down on the bar. "I need a job."

"You chose one helluva way to ask, coming in here and demanding free liquor before noon." Noah folded his arms in front of his chest. "All the bartenders report to Josie. Sure you want to work for your sister?"

Dominic rested his right hand on the bar's polished surface and picked up his coffee with his left hand. "I don't have a choice."

"Your dad would take you back on the force for a while."

"He would, but I can't shoot worth shit right now. And my handwriting is crap. But I can pour a beer and mix a martini."

Noah sighed. "Your resume's better than half my staff. But look, I need to keep this place profitable. It's not just about me."

"It never was. You joined the marines to send money home," Dominic pointed out. "But I get where you're coming from. You have Josie and Isabelle too. And I know my sister still has some debt to pay off. I'm not going to screw up. I'll even bounce for you if you need it."

"I know you can do the job." Noah rested his hands on the bar and leaned forward. "But how long are you going to stay?"

"I'm not going anywhere if I can help it," he said. "As long as Lily's living here, I'm staying."

Noah let out a low whistle. "Things are serious again?"

"No." He took a sip of his coffee. "She kicked me out of her bed and her life."

Noah stared at him and pity lined his furrowed brow. Unable to take it, Dominic held out his shot glass with his right hand. "I need another."

His best friend nodded and picked up the bottle. "She ended things because they caught the guy?"

"You heard about the arrest?" Dominic accepted the glass and poured it down his throat in one swift swallow. Looked as if his damaged hand was good for something after all—taking shots.

And getting Lily off in the bathroom.

"I heard from Josh. He told me that he ran into you two 'celebrating' behind the bar." Noah raised his hands, palms out. "I don't want to hear anymore. I'm just glad you didn't leave the bar in the same state as the staff bathroom."

"It's not the guy." Dominic held up his coffee cup for a refill too and Noah turned around for the pot. "I showed her the mug shot this morning."

With a fresh cup of joe, Dominic gave the down-and-dirty overview of the conversation.

"So she told you to go and you walked out the door? Knowing the guy's still out there?" Noah asked. "Did you leave her with a gun?"

"She can't shoot. Never could. Plus, it's been six weeks. If I think with my brain instead of my . . . If I rely on logic and trust the police report, I know no one's come after her. My dad's still right. It was random, but she's too caught up in the lingering anxiety to realize that now."

"You're willing to risk her safety on that?" Noah demanded.

"I'm not saying I won't drive by her house after I sober up a bit. And again later tonight. Probably again the next day and the one after that. But, man, I need to respect the fact that she is trying to pull her life back together. I want that for her. More than I want to figure out what the hell I'm doing with my life."

Noah nodded. "Sounds like you're working here now. That's a good first step."

"Yeah, it is." But they both knew he needed to heal on the inside. And a big part of that was coming to terms with the fact that he'd never be Lily's hero.

"And you'll still be nearby in case Lily changes her mind," Noah said slowly. "If you're still interested."

Dominic let out a laugh. If he was still interested? He would be *interested* in Lily Greene until he drew his last breath.

"I'll take that as a yes," Noah murmured.

"I'm fucking in love with her," Dominic said. "I always have been. But I keep messing up. And if I have any hope for a future, I need to do this right. I have to earn her trust and hope that she'll fall back in love with me." He looked across the bar at Noah. "I can't afford another mistake. If I get another shot with Lily, I can't fail."

"I'll hire you." Noah ran his hand over his face. "But you need to break the news to your sister. I promised her I'd hire an actual bartender next."

"Thanks." Relief washed over him for the first time since he'd left Lily's house. Or hell, maybe that was the whiskey. But he'd made the first move toward staying. "And I'll talk to Josie."

Noah turned and pulled the bottle of whiskey down. "If you want my advice, you should go back and talk to Lily. Flat out ask her if she loves you. And then, you better prepare her for the fact that you're going to let her down from time to time. You're not perfect."

Dominic flexed his right hand. "Yeah, I'm aware of that."

"This has jack shit to do with your hand. You had

plenty of flaws before you got shot. You were so determined to be the best man you could be for yourself and for Lily that you forgot to be the man Lily needed."

"And you think you know what she needs?" Dominic demanded.

"A man who is willing to fail."

"She already has one of those in her life," Dominic shot back. "Her dad."

Noah shook his head. "From where I'm standing, her father didn't let her down. He never even tried. You came back. And yeah, maybe you messed up. But you can't make mistakes if you never even show up."

The truth sank in and Dominic reached for the bottle. "So you're saying I should go back and try again?"

"Not right away, but yeah." Noah took out a second shot glass and poured a drink. "Give her some space for now. Let her see that she's fine and safe on her own."

Dominic refilled his too. "I'll give her two days. Then I'm going back."

"Good plan. It might help if you clean up a bit. Trim that beard and cut your hair."

Dominic nodded. "I'll need flowers too. Something that doesn't fit down the garbage disposal."

"Can't help you there." Noah raised his glass. "But here's to falling in love and fucking it up."

Dominic lifted his. "To love and failure."

Chapter Fifteen

LILY WATCHED THE sun set from her couch. And her sense of security slipped away with it. But she refused to call Dominic. She would stay awake all night if she had to, but she needed to do this on her own. Face her fears. And she had to win this time.

At midnight, she abandoned her attempts to watch TV. She couldn't hear potential intruders with the volume turned up and the reality show didn't make sense without it. She took out her lesson planner and the classroom roster for the upcoming year. She scanned the names. Three Masons and two Penelopes? Did everyone name their children after the Kardashian kids?

Knock. Knock.

She jumped, sending the paperwork to the floor. Her mother's old clock read one in the morning.

Calm down. Bad guys don't knock.

"Dominic?" she called as she walked through the entryway and headed for the door. Who else would come to her door at this hour?

"No," a familiar and distinctly female voice called back. "But I know where he is."

Lily peered through the peephole and spotted Caroline on the porch. She'd traded her work uniform of baggy shorts and combat boots for fitted blue jeans and sandals. And in her hand she held a square dish.

My backup bodyguard.

She undid the chain and flipped the deadbolt. Her nerves were frayed after hours of trying to convince herself that she was safe, that she didn't need Dominic to feel secure in her own home. She didn't care that it was the middle of the night. She craved the relief of having another person in the house with her.

"I know it's late," Caroline said. "But I have chocolate fudge brownies."

Lily eyed the pan. "Brownies got me into this mess in the first place."

"No, a man hurt you," Caroline said firmly. "Don't take the blame away from him. And whatever you do, don't take it out on the baked goods. They're always on your side."

"You're right." She stepped back and let Caroline into the house.

"But if you're not interested in them," Caroline said as she marched in and scanned the room. Lily had a feeling the former soldier had located the exits and planned routes to them out of habit. "I'll eat while you talk."

"I'm guessing someone told you that I kicked out the last watch dog Noah and Josie sent over?"

Caroline nodded. "From what I understand, Dominic stopped by the bar to ask for a job and he's been taking shots with Noah ever since. When I left, Josie was running the place while her dad watched the baby. I left Josh in charge of the dishwasher and changing kegs. But I'm guessing they've already switched to plastic and the place is in chaos. Josie knows how to serve drinks, but she can't mix them."

"I'd be mad at them for sending you over, but I'm too happy to see you," she admitted.

"They didn't send me. I wanted to talk to you." Caroline lifted the dish just in case Lily's had forgotten about her offering.

"Over brownies. OK." She turned and led the way through the archway and into the living room. "Ignore the mess of paper and make yourself at home. I'll grab the milk."

When she returned, Caroline had the papers arranged in a neat pile and the brownies set out on the coffee table. She had claimed a spot on the floor, close to the treats

"Did Josh make those?" Lily set the milk on the table and followed her late-night guest's lead, settling down on the floor.

Caroline nodded. "When he brought them over, I asked him out on a date."

"Oh, that's great." Lily smiled. She only knew pieces of Caroline's situation, but a date seemed a logical follow-up to a first kiss. "I'm glad you're going to get back out there."

Caroline selected a brownie from the pan. "It's taken me that long to feel ready to share a meal with him. Over a year."

She had to say something. "Noah didn't tell me the details," she said. "But I've heard bits here and there, enough to know—"

"That I was raped?" she said. "That I spent the rest of my deployment looking over my shoulder waiting for my commanding officer to attack me? That I was more afraid of him than the supposed enemy?"

"I didn't . . . I didn't know the details," Lily stammered. "That's awful."

"I thought it would destroy me. But . . ." She plucked a large corner brownie from the pan. "Now I'm going on a date. With a man I like and . . ."

Caroline stared at her brownie as if the baked treat might find the right word for what she felt.

"Desire?" Lily supplied.

"Yes." Caroline looked up at her. "But it took me over a year. And I made a lot of mistakes along the way. There were small victories too. Like the first time I was able to leave the house without pulling my gun on someone."

Lily studied the woman sitting cross-legged on her floor. "Are you armed now?"

"Noah insists on keeping the guns locked up. I had a few setbacks. Just because I left the house once without getting scared and pulling out my weapon didn't mean I could repeat that every day."

Lily nodded. She knew the lesson ran deeper than *don't give Noah's friend firearms*. "So you're saying I should give myself more time? Focus on the small victories. That I shouldn't expect to feel safe and secure on my own this soon?"

Caroline nodded as she took a bite of her brownie. After chasing it with a sip of milk, she added, "That and there is a drunken former ranger at Big Buck's who is madly in love with you. He wants to buy you flowers and he's told anyone who will listen that hell will freeze over before you run them down the garbage disposal."

If Dominic brought her flowers, she would keep them. But it would take a lot more than roses to win her trust and her love now. She'd gone back to him too many times.

"But underneath all his talk," Caroline continued, "I think he might need you as much if not more than you need him."

Lily set her brownie down. "He doesn't—"

"Someone hurt him too," Caroline said quietly. "His bad guy had a gun, not a knife, and Dominic walked into the situation knowing he might be attacked, but that still takes something from you. What it steals? That depends on the person."

Lily stared out into her brightly lit yard. Caroline was right. Dominic had been hurt too. The bad guy with the gun—the terrorist—had stolen away his hopes and dreams for the future. He'd blown away Dominic's identity and left him lost. And after that . . . well, she could forgive him for not coming back to her. Because she knew that it wasn't easy to pull yourself back together. "If we're both so broken, I don't know if we can help each other," she said slowly. "There are things I need from him."

Trust. A promise that he'll stay. . .

"Do you love him?"

She nodded. "I think I always have, even when I was so mad at him I wanted to throw things. But I'm not sure that's enough anymore."

"You don't have to decide now," Caroline said as she nudged the pan toward Lily. "Have another brownie first."

LILY WALKED UP the porch steps cradling a brown paper bag overflowing with school supplies and feeling like she'd won a series of small victories. She'd taken a shower that morning while alone in the house and she hadn't panicked when she'd closed her eyes. At first. She'd opened them too soon and felt the sting of shampoo, but still, one baby step forward.

She'd stopped by the school and chatted with her coworkers—without bumping into Ted, thank goodness. Then she'd gone out to pick up a few extras for her classroom. And the entire time, she'd felt safe and in control.

Her smile faded as soon as she reached the top step and stared at the door. If Dominic were here, he'd go in ahead of her and search her home.

Welcoming him back so that I feel safe—that's not fair to either of us. And I don't think that's love.

But she'd eaten three brownies last night and she still didn't know if the love she felt for Dominic would help her find her way forward—or break her. She didn't want to depend on him—or anyone else—to hold her together.

And while holding boxes of crayons, sheets of stickers, and enough finger paint to redecorate every wall in her house, she couldn't risk falling apart. School started in two weeks. She had to be ready to greet her new class of kindergarten students.

This morning, when she had looked in the mirror, she'd seen only a faint hint of the ugly red cut on her face. One layer of makeup and it disappeared. She would look the part of the calm, welcoming teacher on the first day— as long as the emotional scars didn't betray her.

But what was the worst that could happen? She would ask her assistant to take over the class while she took a quick break for a panic attack? And what could possibly set her off at the school? She'd always felt safe there. She didn't need a former soldier checking behind her class-room door or looking under the child-sized desks.

She shifted the bag to her right arm and reached into the pocket of her capri-length pink pants for her keys. Today was a day for victories. Her bright white short-sleeve shirt, her pink pants, every piece of her day screamed sunshine and success. And when she unlocked the door, when she walked inside, she would be fine—

"Ms. Greene? Lily Greene?"

Her hand froze in her pocket. Panic surged at the sound of that familiar voice. She'd heard it twice before. The memories came rushing back, two pieces of a puzzle she hadn't been able to connect until now. *You ruined everything*—what the man currently standing on her porch said to her the day he sliced her arms, her face, and her stomach. The day he cut away her confidence in the world around her. And *Ms. Greene, I'm here to pick up my son.*

She closed her eyes. She didn't need Dominic watching over her at the elementary school. She needed him here. Now. Hearing that voice, she knew her reasons for sending him away were foolish. She would trust Dominic to save her life, always and forever.

I need him to save me right now!

But he wasn't here. And that wasn't his failure. It was hers. She'd cast him away. There was no one here to help her now. No one to keep her safe. She would need to do it herself.

"Ms. Greene, I need to talk to you."

She couldn't move. She didn't want to see him again.

"Turn around and talk to me!" he barked. Anger and desperation seeped through his words.

She wanted to run away. But she knew she wouldn't win by trying to escape. If he'd dared to approach her again, she doubted he'd come empty handed.

Slowly, her arm tightening around the school supplies, she turned and faced the man who'd haunted her nightmares for the past six weeks.

"Mr. Stanton," she said, looking first at his familiar dark brown eyes, the ones she'd expected to see on the mug shot Dominic handed her. But that didn't matter now. Whether she was right . . . none of it mattered. Because this time Louis Stanton wasn't wielding a knife.

This time he had a gun.

The minutes seemingly slowed as she watched the man with the lethal weapon stand on her front porch in broad daylight and demand to talk to her.

"How can I help you?" Her shaking voice betrayed the imminent, pulse-pounding fear that her next breath would be her last. Any moment, he would pull the trigger. Any second—

"Open the door," he said. He wasn't shouting now, but the note of desperation remained. And it sent a chill down her spine. "I need to talk to you inside," he added.

She gave a curt nod. "I have to unlock the door."

"Now," he growled.

She saw the tension ripple through his forearm. And she dropped the bag of school supplies. Small containers of plastic finger paint rolled over the wooden boards. Crayons spilled out of boxes. And sheets of *Great Job!* and *You're a Star!* stickers stared up at her.

She reached into her pocket and withdrew her keychain. Her hand shook and she approached the lock. But she managed to insert the key. As she turned it, she realized that if she survived, she would never feel safe again. Not on the street, in the park, at her home, or even in the classroom where she'd planned to hand out the *You're a Star!* stickers.

But her safety had always been an illusion. Her sense of security could be ripped away in an instant. She'd been so determined to heal after her first encounter with Mr. Stanton that she hadn't realized she'd been holding out for something she didn't really need. There was only one thing this man could never take from her.

Love.

She'd been a fool not to fall back in love with Dominic, to hold tight to him, and fight for an imperfect future with him.

She stepped into the hall and stole a quick glance at the wall Dominic had pressed her up against only a few days ago.

"Ms. Greene."

She turned to face the man who'd uprooted her life. He'd closed the door behind him, leaving the school supplies strewn across her porch. But he didn't bother turning the lock.

Sweat beaded on his forehead. And for the first time, she noticed his suit and tie. Even his black dress shoes shone as if he'd polished them that morning. Had he dressed up for this? To come here and kill her?

"I need to talk to you," he continued. His voice shook, but his hand holding the gun remained steady.

Dominic, Noah, Ryan—they'd logged hours at the gun range. But she'd only held a gun once. She could tell the difference between the small handgun in Louis Stanton's hand and a hunting rifle. But beyond that, she didn't have a clue. Had Louis released the safety? Did his weapon even have one? How could she stop him from pulling the trigger?

"I need your help," he said.

Her world felt as if it had turned over. It was no longer a question of whether she'd been right about her attacker returning for her. Or if the police, Dominic's father, and even Dominic were correct in assuming the man who'd cut her in the park was crazy. They'd all been right. Louis Stanton had been after her. It wasn't random. And he was nuts.

"But . . ." she sputtered. "You attacked—"

"I was angry."

No kidding.

"They're going to take him away. My son. And it's your fault." He spoke as if he were accusing her of taking his parking place. His voice remained calm and clear. The same tone he'd used when she'd handed him the forms to file with the front office if he wished to pick up his child . . .

"Mr. Stanton, there's nothing I can do." Her tone mirrored his surreal calm as if she could talk her way out of this, as if he wasn't pointing a gun at her in her own home. "I don't know anything about custody—"

"Call the judge," he demanded. "Now. Tell her you were wrong. Tell her I never tried to take my son from school. I didn't violate the custody agreement. I wasn't trying to kidnap him. I didn't try to see him without a court-appointed supervisor!"

Her eyes widened. "Mr. Stanton—"

"It's all lies," he snapped. "You have to tell the judge. She's deciding today. I know she's going to take my ex's side. They're saying I tried to kidnap him from school and from the playground. I took him out of state once, but . . . I didn't kidnap my son. He's *mine*."

His emphasis on the last word made her shudder.

"I can't go back there until you fix what you started,"

he added. "My bitch of an ex started petitioning the judge again after I showed up at school. You told her I'd been there."

If she hadn't told her student's mom, Lily bet her son would have said something. But Mr. Stanton blamed her. He was holding her at gunpoint in the middle of the day while dressed in a suit.

And now it became clear. The suit and tie. The polished shoes. He'd been at the courthouse.

"They'll take him away for good." He pointed the gun at her head. "But if you call—"

She felt tears well in her eyes. "Mr. Stanton, there is nothing I can do."

"Call," he barked.

Oh God, what would Dominic do? Fight him? She didn't have the strength. Or would Dominic pretend to make the call? Was this man so crazed he wouldn't realize she'd dialed for help and not the courthouse? And if he did?

Did it matter? He'd beaten her and cut her up with a knife in a fit of rage. He blamed her for losing a child he should never be allowed near.

The child.

Jay Stanton was a shy boy who loved to color, play on the slides at recess, and hated everything about frogs, even pictures of them. He'd brought a tuna fish sandwich and a yogurt for lunch every day last year. He spoke with a slight lisp. And he'd been in her care, her student, for an entire year.

"OK. I'll call," she said. But her cell phone was in her purse, which was lying beneath a pile of stickers and crayon boxes on the porch. "My landline is in the kitchen."

She took a step back and Louis nodded. She kept walking, her eyes on his gun as she made her way into the kitchen. She needed to make that call. Her safety came second to that little boy's future. If Louis Stanton shot her, walked out of here and back into that courtroom, if by some horrible twist of fate the judge granted him access to Jay . . .

"Do you have the number?" she asked.

He reached in his pocket and withdrew a slip of paper. Of course he'd brought the contact information. He was crazy, but clearly on a mission. He held it out to her and she took it, careful not to touch his hand. One touch and she might lose her nerve and start screaming, begging, and trying to run away.

She picked up the cordless phone. She looked at the number scrawled on the paper, then drew a deep breath and dialed Big Buck's Bar.

"Hello, this is—"

"Is this the Forever courthouse?" She spoke fast, talking over the man on the other end. If the words "Big Buck's" carried through the receiver, if Louis Stanton realized she'd called for help . . .

"I need the family court division."

"Lily?"

She heard the shock in Dominic's tone and pressed

forward. "The extension is three, three, two? Could you, um, connect me?"

Her voice faltered over the words. She closed her eyes and hoped the man she'd kicked out of her house got the message and rushed to her rescue.

Chapter Sixteen

FUCK THE FLOWERS.

Dominic dropped the phone. By the time it hit the rubber mat, he'd vaulted over the bar's polished surface.

"Lily needs help," he called to Noah as he pushed through the customers. "Call my dad. Call the station. It has something to do with the family court in town."

He'd reached the door and had his hand on the knob. *Three, three, two?* What the hell did those numbers mean? Where was she? Not at the courthouse, if she was pretending to call. Her house? She lived at number sixty-eight. Hell, he'd memorized her address in high school along with her home phone number.

Three, three, two—the first three digits on her home phone number.

"She's at home," he added. And then he ran out the door and headed for his rental. But Caroline beat him to the driver's side door.

"Take this." She thrust a pistol into his hand. "It's loaded with a round in the chamber."

"Thanks." He didn't have time to ask questions and figure out if she'd broken into Noah's gun safe. He climbed into the car and peeled out of the parking lot.

Please let there be a cop between here and there. He'd lead them right to her damn house. If the man who'd attacked Lily in the park was with her, if he was hurting her, Dominic needed backup. Hell, he wanted the whole damn police force with him. Otherwise he was going in with a gun, one good hand, and the determination to bust in there and save her.

I can't let her down.

The stakes were too damn high. If she died, if that bastard killed her because he hadn't believed her when she'd told him again and again that she'd been targeted . . .

But he had been on her side. Until he'd started to doubt his judgment and wonder if he'd been blinded by fucking love.

Still, he'd looked into her list. He'd used his dad's computer—and the police department's resources—to search for anything he could find on the list of names.

Which one has a connection to family court?

The peanut butter dad was a certified ass, but from everything he'd dug up on the family, the man's wife was his perfect match.

Dominic accelerated down the familiar stretch of road leading to Lily's quiet neighborhood. Family court. The dad who didn't have the correct paperwork to pick up his son . . .

Louis Stanton.

He turned on her street and mentally ran through everything he knew about Louis Stanton. Nine years at a desk job outside of town. He was laid off about a year ago. His wife kicked him out, filed for divorce and sole custody. She'd won. Louis moved back to Washington to live with his uncle. He'd secured a new job that paid well. Apart from being dealt a rough blow when he lost his job, Louis Stanton was a model citizen. He didn't even have a parking ticket. The man was a getting his life back.

But not his son.

Dominic slammed on the brakes and put the car in park. He didn't know why Louis thought Lily held the key to getting his son back. But any man who'd attack a woman was crazy in his book.

A patch of red on the white porch steps caught his eye. *Not Lily. Oh God, please not Lily.*

He was out of the car, running for the house before he saw the bottles strewn about the porch. Boxes of crayons spilled everywhere. There was a patch of blue in the corner. Hell, it wasn't blood. It was finger paint.

He pushed open the door and fought like hell to control his ragged breathing. All those years of training, all that time spent away from the woman he loved trying to make himself better, hoping to come home her hero— this was his chance. Now he needed to execute as if he were a mission.

He raised the gun, his right index finger wrapped around the trigger. Silently, he moved into the entryway and scanned the space. She wasn't here. But—

"I swear I'm on hold."

He heard Lily voice, firm and fearful. *But fucking alive.* And he headed for the kitchen. He stopped beside the wine cabinet in her living room. The archway leading to the kitchen stood a few inches in front of him. He could see Louis from his vantage point, but Lily was out of sight.

Where was her phone? He tried to picture the room. The coffeepot in the far corner by the sink . . . The window above the sink looking out the side of the house . . . The phone by the fridge, which stood on the opposite wall.

"It's been fifteen minutes," Louis Stanton said. And damn, his voice sounded a helluva lot more panicked than Lily's. "I need to get back there."

The man directing a pistol at Lily looked down at his watch. Dominic needed to move now. He glanced down at the gun in his right hand.

At this distance, he could hit Louis and disarm him *if* his finger pulled the trigger. And there was no guarantee his damaged nerves would receive the signal and follow orders. He silently switched the gun to his left hand. He could make the shot at this distance. Hell, he didn't have a choice. He couldn't fail her. Not here. Not now.

"I need to be back to the courthouse in ten minutes," Louis said as if timing was his big fucking problem, not the fact that he was holding a woman at gunpoint.

Dominic took advantage of the other man's momentary distraction and stepped into the room, with his weapon raised and prepared to fire.

But dammit, nervous and terrified Louis Stanton

moved first. The bastard stepped toward Lily. He held the gun up to her face and said, "Give me the phone."

He saw the panic in Lily's eyes. Dominic didn't have a clue who was on the other end of that line. Noah? Caroline? It sure as hell wasn't a representative from family court.

But he also saw her blue eyes widen as she spotted him. Her lips parted as if she might call out. He shook his head and hoped she got the message.

"Give me the phone," Louis repeated, waving his gun-free hand in the air like an impatient child.

Dominic didn't have a choice right now. He had to reveal his position. And he couldn't do it by firing at Louis. Not while the bastard stood in front of Lily.

If he missed, if he hit her . . .

Not an option.

"Louis," he called.

The man who'd hurt Lily, who'd hunted her down and held a fucking gun to her head, turned. He looked crazed and pretty damn surprised to see a gun pointed in *his* direction. But still Dominic didn't fire. He couldn't take advantage of the other man's shock with Lily so close. He didn't have the accuracy.

"Lily! Move!" he barked. *Please listen to me, honey. Please trust me. Give me a second chance and even if I can't win your heart, I'll keep it beating.*

She obeyed. Thank fucking God. She dove for the floor at the foot of the refrigerator, her arms raised to cover her head.

Dominic spared her one last glimpse. The long blond

hair. The faded marks on her forearms. Her blue eyes wide with fear. He loved her. He would always love her.

Then he turned his attention back to Louis. He aimed and he pulled the trigger.

And so did the man trembling in his shoes.

Dominic's shoulder exploded with pain. It was on fire. And fuck a duck. It was his right arm. As he fell to the kitchen floor, he turned away from the man who'd dropped like a stone and looked at the woman he loved.

"I had to, Lily," he murmured. He saw tears streaming down her face. "I love you too much to let him hurt you."

Chapter Seventeen

LILY CRAWLED ACROSS the floor. Her entire body shook from the roller-coaster ride of fear. The gun aimed at her, the sound of Dominic on the phone, the wondering if that would be the last time she heard his voice, if the madman with the gun would shoot her first . . .

"Dominic," she whispered as she reached his side. He turned his head toward her, his green eyes open and alert.

Oh, thank goodness.

"Is he moving?" he asked.

She stole a brief glance at the other body sprawled on the floor. Louis Stanton's right hand was open and his gun rested on the floor a few feet away. She watched his fingers, waiting for them to reach for his weapon, to try to hurt her again, to take more from them . . . And nothing. Not a twitch.

"No," she said, turning her attention back to Dominic.

Her gaze traveled south to his black Big Buck's T-shirt. The right side looked wet. And below his shoulder, blood pooled, seeping out from beneath him.

"You're bleeding," she said.

"Gunshot," he said. "And it had to be my right shoulder."

Oh God.

"I need to call an ambulance," she whispered.

"On their way. I had Noah call the cavalry when I left. My dad's probably leading the charge . . ."

"They'll be here soon," she said, trying for reassuring. It wasn't a question. The paramedics needed to get there. He needed help. They had to save him.

She stared at the blood, her mind racing through the first-aid course she took every year as part of her teacher training. Gunshot wound. Lots of blood. Apply pressure. Soak up the blood.

Hands still trembling, she pulled off her white shirt and pressed it against the wound on his chest. "That's better," she murmured as the fabric turned pink, then red as the color spread.

"Thanks for calling me," he said, his lips curved into a smile.

His lips . . . She could see his mouth. A thin layer of stubble covered his jawline.

"You trimmed your beard," she muttered. The mundane fact, so unimportant to whether he lived or died . . . but she couldn't stop looking. Not that it mattered if he had a beard a mile long or not. She loved him.

He chuckled. Then he grimaced as if laughing delivered a strong dose of pain. "Noah said you'd like this better. I also wanted to bring you flowers. Today. Later. I was . . ." He drew a sharp inhale.

"Dominic, please—" She glanced down at her hands, now covered in his blood as she pressed her shirt to his wound. The white fabric was bright red. He needed an ambulance. *Now.*

"I was giving you time." He managed the words through ragged gasps for air. "And space."

She raised an eyebrow. "Two days?" She'd kicked him out, yet this time he planned to spin around and come back to her. He'd respected her request, but he hadn't disappeared for good. Maybe he couldn't. Maybe he'd meant it when he said he loved her . . .

"I know," he muttered. "I waited too long. But it was Noah's idea. Blame him. And I still—" He inhaled sharply. "I still drove by every morning and every night. Last night I came by five times. I'm sorry, Lil. I know you wanted . . . wanted me to stay . . . away . . ."

He drew another ragged breath.

"Shh," she murmured. Outside she heard the sirens growing closer and closer. It was her turn to laugh as relief seeped in. Help was coming. "They'll be here soon."

"Noah told me to tell you I'll mess up," Dominic whispered. "Again and again. In the future . . . I'll keep fucking up, Lil. Noah knows it . . . I know it . . ."

Mess up?

"You saved me," she said firmly. "If you hadn't rushed in . . ."

Louis Stanton had hurt her once. This time, he might

have killed her. If Louis had discovered that she'd called a bar instead of the courthouse . . .

"I had to, Lil."

"They're almost here," she said. "The paramedics. You're going to be OK. They'll help—"

"I'll be fine."

She nodded, clinging to his certainty even though the blood beneath her hands told a different story. The sirens stopped in front of her house and she glanced at the door.

"Look at me, Lily."

She tore her attention away from the rush of footsteps on her front steps and focused on his pale, oh-so-familiar face, his deep green eyes.

"I'm not leaving you, Lily. Not this time. Not ever again if I can help it." His eyes closed. "But I might . . . I might need a little . . . nap."

The paramedics burst in as the love of her life passed out on her kitchen floor.

"Help him," she begged, tears rushing freely down her face now. "Please, help him!"

Hands wrapped around her bare shoulders and drew her away from Dominic. "You can ride with him, ma'am," a deep voice promised. "But let us take care of him now."

She wrapped her arms around her waist and watched. More bodies filled the room. Men and women in uniforms. Forever's chief of police rushed in and the sea of people parted for him.

"Lily, you're all right," Dominic's father said, his expression transitioning to relief. Then he looked down at his son. "Oh God. Oh no. Dominic."

"He was hit in the shoulder," one of the paramedics called as they prepared to carry him out to the waiting ambulance.

The chief of police nodded, his jaw tight. "Exit wound?"

"Yes, sir. Close range. We'll know more when we get to the hospital."

And they carried Dominic out. She stepped forward and a woman, also in uniform, handed her a shirt. "For the ride to the hospital."

Lily nodded and pulled it over her head. Behind her, she heard Chief Fairmore ask: "And the suspect?"

"He's dead, sir."

Lily walked out of the kitchen. It was over. The man who'd hurt her, who'd left her living in fear, he was dead. She walked faster, stepping over the paint and stickers still covering her front porch. She needed to get to Dominic. She had to be there when he woke up. She had to tell him the words she should have said when he'd first come home, or later when he'd stood in her kitchen and told her that he loved her.

She climbed into the ambulance and moved to the side, allowing the paramedics to do their work. But once they pulled away, sirens blaring, she leaned forward and pressed her lips to his ear. And she whispered, "I love you, Dominic Fairmore."

DOMINIC WOKE UP to a chorus of beeping machines. He felt like he'd been dragged back in time. He blinked, studying the hospital ceiling, trying to orient himself. He'd been shot again. Only this time, he was in Oregon. And this wasn't a military hospital.

"You're awake?"

He turned his head and saw the woman he'd rushed to save. Lily. His Lily. Unharmed. She'd pulled her blond hair back into a ponytail. Her familiar blue eyes were red and puffy as if she'd been crying. And she was wearing an oversized navy T-shirt that read "Forever, Oregon, EMS Squad" with bright pink bloodstained pants. But still, she looked so damn beautiful.

"Hey." His voice felt rusty and unused. He tried to reach for the water pitcher and paper cups on the bedside table, but Lily moved faster. She poured a cup and held it to his lips as he drank.

"Was I out long?" he rasped.

She smiled. "You slept for ten straight hours."

"Huh. It must be the painkillers." He could see the IV. Plus, he knew his shoulder should be hurting a lot more than it did. He looked at her over the rim of water cup.

"The nurses and I have been taking bets—painkillers or caffeine withdrawal. I had the advantage. I know your coffee habit. But the overnight nurse was on my side too."

"Don't tell me you spent the entire time sitting is that chair and watching me sleep."

She shrugged. "It was my turn. Everyone was here earlier, when you came out of surgery. Your dad. Josie and Noah. Even Caroline. They saw you muttering and asking the nurse for coffee. She said you needed sleep. So I sent everyone home."

"You could have gone home too," he said.

"I needed to talk to you." She placed her hand on top of his. "I was wrong, Dominic."

He raised an eyebrow. "I was going to tell you the same thing. All that time you were convinced someone was after you, that it wasn't random. I should have listened."

"Maybe you will next time," she said. "But I wasn't talking about Louis Stanton. I was wrong to send you away. I thought I needed safety, security, trust—"

"You deserve all those things, honey," he said, the raspy quality slipping from his voice.

"But I *need* you." She looked him straight in the eyes. "Your love."

"You have it," he said. "Always have, even when I tried to stay away and make room for someone better, who would never let you down."

"You won't," she said firmly.

"Lil—"

"Dominic, you're my rock. My stability. My safety net. And yes, I might need you to check behind every door for the rest of my life. After yesterday, I might never feel safe again."

Don't say that. But he knew it was the truth and he didn't want any lies between them. He wanted to be the one person in Forever, the one person in this world, she shared everything with—her feelings, her body, and her love.

"Or maybe in a year," she added, "I'll be able to close

my eyes in the shower even when you're not home. Or maybe not. I'm done giving my fear a timeline."

He nodded. "That's good, Lily. Really good. And I'll be there. When you shower, when you sleep. I swear I'll be there for you."

He'd play the part of her bodyguard forever if that's what she needed. He wanted more, so damn much more . . . But maybe they weren't ready yet. Still too broken. Hell, he didn't even know if his right arm worked anymore.

"And if you do decide to leave—

"I'm not going anywhere, Lily."

"But if you change your mind, if you go back to the army, or to Georgia, I'll follow," she continued, pushing on with a speech that he suspected she'd been preparing for the last ten hours while he'd taken an extended stay in dreamland.

"I'll go wherever you go," she said. "But not because you make me feel safe."

He sat up a little straighter at those words.

"Dominic Fairmore, you're everything I need." She inhaled and he swore he saw tears brimming in her blue eyes, threatening to flood her cheeks.

"Don't cry, Lil."

"Shut up." She wiped her eyes with her free hand. "I'm trying to tell you how I feel."

He fell silent. *Ask her if she loves you.* And he would. He'd follow Noah's advice if she didn't say the words. But he knew her answer didn't matter. Even if she wasn't in love with him, he would still stand by her, watch over her, and take a bullet for her. He loved her too damn much to walk away ever again.

"I love you, Dominic."

Fuck, yes.

Relief, joy, and yeah, in spite of the pain meds, desire surged through him. Lily Fairmore, his high school sweetheart, the only woman he'd ever wanted, ever loved or made love to, she loved him. Hell, he'd take another bullet right here, right now, just to hear her say those words again.

"I love you too, honey." He reached his good hand up and cupped her cheek. "I always have and I always will."

Epilogue

_____

One year later. . .

"LILY? ARE YOU ready?" Dominic paced back and forth in front of the door to the Big Buck's bathroom. "Noah will get suspicious if I don't get back out there soon."

"Almost," the woman he loved called back.

Dominic paused by the door's edge. He glanced over his shoulder but the bar's back room remained blissfully empty. No sign of Caroline yet. They hadn't even opened for business. But Noah had asked him to come in early and help add a fresh coat of polish to the bar top today. And how the hell was his best friend supposed to know that Lily would need him in the middle of a Wednesday? Dominic had started paying attention to the calendar and even he hadn't realized that they'd hit their window.

Of course he wasn't the one taking his temperature all the time, waiting and hoping the timing would be just right . . .

"Lily, honey, if you're taking the time to paint your nails to match your panties," he murmured through the closed door, "you can stop right now. I can perform on demand."

And yeah, that was an understatement. He'd been hard since she called. Maybe not from that exact moment. At first, he'd worried that she was sitting in her car too afraid to go into her house—now their home. But it had been months since she'd been paralyzed with fear. Still, he knew that it would always linger. He couldn't erase it. But he sure as hell could drop everything and help her deal with it.

But then she'd informed him that she would be swinging by the bar. Oh, and by the way, would he meet her in the staff bathroom . . . and please don't tell Noah . . .

"I know you can perform when needed," she whispered. She opened the door and let him slip inside. "But you shouldn't have to. I want this to be special."

Dominic stared at the gorgeous blonde in hot pink lace panties and nothing else. "It doesn't get much better than this," he murmured, looking her up and down. And yeah, her toenails matched her underwear. "But, Lil, you can seduce me another time. Right now, we need to make a baby."

And then I need to get back to work before Noah realizes what we're doing back here.

"But I want to seduce you now." Lily reached for his waistline and began releasing his jeans. He raised his left hand to help as she lowered the zipper. She guided his pants over his hips, taking his underwear with them. Finally she freed the part of him that planned to take center stage in the baby making process—and love every minute of it.

But instead of resting her perfect backside on the vanity's edge and spreading her legs wide to take him in, Lily bent at the waist and captured his eager erection in his mouth.

"Ah hell," he groaned. "Lily—"

She pulled back. Her lips hovered over him as her hand ran up and down his hard length. "I believe I owe you a demonstration of my super-special oral skills. This time without interruption."

"Here?" he rasped. "Now? Lily, Noah's in the other room waiting."

"I could put a sign outside that says 'Blow Job in Progress.'"

"Yeah, Noah would love that."

She returned her mouth to his dick and he forgot all about his best friend, the bar, the reason they were in this bathroom in the middle of the day . . . His world narrowed to Lily. Her mouth, her hands . . . and he had to have her.

She drew back again, but he could feel her breath as

she spoke. "I want to make you lose control. I don't want you to hold back. Not this time."

Desire roared through him as he hauled her up. "Enough, Lily. You want wild? Rough? You've got it. I can't hold back any longer."

His hands gripped the back of her thighs as he lifted her up. He felt her legs wrap around his waist. And he thrust into her.

I'm home.

It didn't matter where they were—their bed, this bathroom, the backseat of his truck—this was his home and his refuge. Lily. His love. His wife. And one day, the future mother of his child.

He drove into her, harder and faster, determined to give her what she wanted, to make her dreams for a baby come true. Her backside began to slide on the vanity. And he lifted her off. He turned and pressed her up against the windowless wall. And yeah, it was a damn good thing they'd never bothered to decorate the walls, or pictures would be tumbling to the ground right about now.

With his fingers pressed into her ass, he thrust harder and faster, driving them closer and closer . . .

"Oh my!" She threw her head back and hit the wall. He buried himself inside her, his hips forcing hers into the physical barrier at her back. He felt it give a little, the walls crumbling, giving way to the power of his need to fuck her, claim her, love her.

"Dominic!" She screamed his name over and over, her body convulsing around him as she came.

And he followed her, moaning the only words that

mattered as he came inside her. "I love you, Lily. I fuck-ing love you."

Slowly, he stopped thrusting. The last trace of plea-sure faded from his grateful cock. But the love—the love stayed, pulsing through him as he held her against the broken bathroom wall.

"I think that might be it," she murmured, resting her head back against the cracked surface. Hell, he'd need to replace the sheetrock this time. Noah wouldn't be happy about that. But Dominic didn't give a damn. Right now, the woman in his arms trumped everything.

"Honey, you can seduce me anytime. I want to make your dreams come true. I want this baby as much as you do."

She tilted her head and looked at him, her blue eyes sparkling with mischief.

Give me ten minutes and I'll show you again.

"Dominic?"

"Yeah, honey?" He lowered his mouth to hers, steal-ing a kiss. With her cheeks flushed, hell, he couldn't get enough of her. He never would.

"I might have lied to you."

Bullshit. They never held anything back. Not any-more. "Might have?" he murmured, raising an eyebrow.

"My temperature's not perfect," she admitted. "I needed to see you. I wanted everything to be perfect, but I couldn't wait until after your shift."

"Were you scared?" he asked, concern trumping his desire. "If you are, I can come to you. Anytime."

"No, not scared." Her mischievous grin widened. "But I couldn't wait until tonight to tell you."

"Tell me what?" His grip tightened, unwilling to let her go. His pulse quickened and his excitement rose even if another part of him was still too relaxed to participate yet.

"I took a test this morning. A pregnancy test. And this time . . . Dominic, it was positive." Her voice held a world of wonder. "I wanted to be sure, so I used the entire box. All positive."

"You're pregnant." Saying the words out loud brought a fever pitch of happiness he'd never imagined. "We're having a baby?"

She nodded.

A baby. Their baby. Her dream come true. And now his.

"I love you, Lily. And I'm going to love our baby too." He felt the joy rush in on the heels of pure awe. And he realized that he'd never believed he would get here. He'd never believed he would be good enough for not only Lily, but the promise of a child.

"Everything all right in there?" Noah's voice cut through the perfection.

"Great," Dominic called back as he ran his hand down Lily's hair. "I'm great."

And that was a fucking understatement. He felt like his heart might explode with love. The rangers, his team, and the success he'd thought he needed to claim his sweet, sexy Lily—it felt like another lifetime. This was his future. Lily. A baby. A family.

"Yeah, well, I saw Lily's car out front," Noah said. "So I know you're not taking apart the bathroom on your own. Take your time. I'm going to head out for a while."

Dominic waited until he heard the door slam shut. Then he placed his hand over her stomach. "I'm going to be there for our child. I'll love this baby, Lil. With all my heart."

"I know you will." She rose up and brushed her lips over his. "And I know you're staying this time. I know it in my heart."

"Damn right I'm staying. For the baby. And for you, Lil. Always for you." Then he dropped to his knees, ignoring the broken bits of wall on the floor. "Spread your legs, honey. And let me show you how much I love you, now and forever."

Sara Jane Stone continues
her devastatingly sexy
Second Shot series with

MIXING TEMPTATION

After a year spent living in hiding—with no
end in sight—Caroline Andrews wants to
reclaim her life. But the lingering trauma from
her days serving with the marines leaves her
afraid to trust the tempting logger who delivers
friendship and the promise of something more.

Following an accident that nearly robbed him of
his hopes for the future, Josh Summers believes
life has given him a second chance. He wants
to settle down with the woman who stole his
attention and his heart. And he's willing to wait
until she's ready to be more than "just friends."
When fear of discovery leaves Caroline pretending
to be his date, Josh tempts her to try the real
thing—a relationship built on trust, not lies.

But then the past threatens and Caroline
must risk everything—including her
freedom—to bury her demons before she
can take a chance on happy-ever-after.

MIXING TEMPTATION

After a year spent living in hiding—with no
end in sight—Caroline Andrews wants to
reclaim her life. But the lingering trauma from
her day at every turn with the marines faces her
afraid to trust the tempting logger who delivers
friendship and the promise of something more.

Following an accident that nearly robbed him of
his hopes for the future, Josh Summers believes
life has given him a second chance. He wants
to settle down with the woman who stole his
attention and his heart. And he's willing to wait
until she's ready to be more than "just friends."
When fear of discovery leaves Caroline pretending
to be his date, Josh tempts her to try the real
thing—a relationship built on trust, not lies.

But then the past threatens and Caroline
must risk everything—including her
freedom—to bury her demons before she
can take a chance on happily ever after.

And keep reading for an excerpt
from the first book
in the *Second Shot* series,

SERVING TROUBLE

Five years ago, Josie Fairmore left timber
country in search of a bright future. Now she's
back home with a mountain of debt and reeling
from a loss that haunts her. Desperate for a
job, she turns to the one man she wishes she
could avoid. The man who rocked her world one
wild night and then walked right out of it.

Former Marine Noah Tager is managing his
dad's bar and holding tight to the feeling that
his time overseas led to failure. The members of
his small town think he's a war hero, but after
everything he's witnessed, Noah doesn't want
a pat on the back. The only thing he desires is a
second chance with his best friend's little sister.

Josie's determined to hold on to her heart
and not repeat her mistakes, but when
danger arrives on Noah's doorstep and
takes aim at Josie, they just might discover
that sometimes love is worth the risk.

An Excerpt from

SERVING TROUBLE

"I DROVE TO the wrong bar."

Josie Fairmore stared up at the unlit sign towering above the nearly vacant parking lot, her cell phone pressed to her ear. Nothing changed in Forever, Oregon. Everything from the people to the names of the bars remained the same. The triplets, who had to be over a hundred now, still owned The Three Sisters Café downtown. Every car and truck she'd sped past had the high school football team's flag mounted on the roof or featured on the bumper. And her father was still the chief of police.

Nothing changed. That was why she'd left for college and never looked back.

Until now.

She'd blown past the Forever town line ten minutes ago. She'd driven straight to the place that promised a rescue from her current hell. And she'd parked under the sign, which appeared determined to prove her wrong.

"Josephine Fairmore, it is ten thirty in the morning," Daphne said through the phone, her tone oddly stern for the owner of a strip club situated outside the town limits. "The fact that you're at a bar might be your first mistake."

Damn. If the owner of The Lost Kitten was her voice of reason, Josie was screwed.

"When did they take the 'country' out of Big Buck's Country Bar?" Josie stared at the letters above the entrance to the town's oldest bar. She twirled the key to her red Mini, which looked out of place beside the lone monster truck in the lot. She should probably take the car back to the city. The Mini didn't belong in the land of four-wheelers, pickups, and logging trucks. The red car would miss the parking garage.

But I can't afford the parking garage anymore. I can't even pay my rent. Or my bills. . .

"Big Buck gave in three years ago," Daphne explained, drawing Josie's attention back to the bar parking lot. "He decided to take Noah's advice and get rid of the mechanical bull. He wanted to attract the college crowd."

"He got rid of the bull before I went to college." And before his son left to join the United States Marine Corps. She should know. She'd ridden the bull at his going away party.

With Noah.

And then she'd ridden Noah.

"Well, Buck made a few more changes," Daphne said. "He added a new sound system and—"

"He changed the name. I guess that explains why Noah came home." She glanced at the dark, quiet bar. The hours posted by the door read "Open from noon until the cows come home (or 3am, whichever comes first!)."

"He served for five years and did two tours in Afghanistan. Stop by The Three Sisters and you'll get an earful about his heroics," Daphne said. "But from what I've heard, Noah didn't want to sign up for another five. Not after his grandmother died last year."

"You've seen him?" Josie looked down at her cowboy boots. She hadn't worn them since that night in Noah's barn. She'd thought they'd help her land the job at the "country" bar. But now she wished she'd worn her Converse, maybe a pair of heels.

"Yes."

"At The Lost Kitten?" Why, after all this time, after she never responded to his apologetic letter, would she care if Noah spent his free time watching women strip off their clothes? One wild, stupid, naked night cut short by her big brother didn't offer a reason for jealousy.

But the fact that I told him I love him? That might.

"No. I bumped into him at the café." Daphne hesitated. "He didn't smile. Not once."

"PTSD?" she asked quietly. She couldn't imagine walking into a war zone and leaving without long-lasting trauma. The things he probably saw . . .

"Maybe," Daphne said. "But he's not jumpy. He just seems pissed off at the world. Elvira was behind the counter that day. She tried to thank him for serving our country after he ordered a burger. He set a ten on the counter and walked out before his food arrived."

"He left his manners in the Middle East." Josie stared at the door to Big Buck's. "Might hurt my chances for getting a job."

"I think your lack of waitressing or bartending experience will be the nail in the coffin. But if Noah turns you down, you can work here."

"I'd rather keep my shirt on while I work," Josie said dryly.

And he won't turn me down. He promised to help me.

But that was before he turned into a surly former marine.

"You'd make more without it," Daphne said. "Or you can tell the hospital, the collection agency—whoever's coming after you—the truth. You're broke."

"I did. They gave me a payment plan and I need to stick to it." She headed for the door. "I ignored those bills for months. Besides, what kind of mother doesn't pay her child's medical bills?"

The kind who buried her son twenty-seven days after he was born.

Daphne didn't say the words, but Josie knew she was thinking them. Her best friend was the only person in Forever who knew the truth about why she was desperate for a paycheck. If only Daphne had inherited a restaurant or a bookstore—a place with fully clothed employees.

"He has to agree," Josie added. "I need that money."

"I know." Daphne sighed. "And I need to get to work. I

have a staff of topless waitresses and dancers who depend on me for their paycheck. Good luck, Josie."

"Thanks." She ended the call and slipped her phone into the bag slung over her shoulder alongside her wallet and resume.

She drew a deep breath. But a churning feeling started in her belly, foreboding, threatening. She knew this feeling and she didn't like it. Something bad always followed.

Her boyfriend headed for the door convinced he was too young for a baby . . . Her water broke too early. . .

She tried the door. Locked, dammit.

Ignoring the warning bells in her head telling her to run to her best friend's club and offer to serve a topless breakfast, she raised her hand and knocked.

"Hang on a sec," a deep voice called from the other side. She remembered that sound and could hear the echo of his words from five long years ago, before he'd joined the marines and before she'd gone to college hoping for a brighter future—and found more heartache.

Call, email, or send a letter. Hell, send a carrier pigeon. I don't care how you get in touch, or where I am. If you need me, I'll find a way to help.

He'd meant every word. But people changed. They hardened. They took hits and got back up, leaving their heart beaten and wrecked on the ground.

She glanced down as if the bloody pieces of her broken heart would appear at her feet. Nope. Nothing but cement and her boots. She'd left her heart behind in Portland, dead and buried, thank you very much.

The door opened. She looked up and . . .

Oh my . . . Wow. . .

She'd gained five pounds—well, more than that, but she'd lost the rest. She'd cried for weeks, tears running down her cheeks while she slept, and flooding her eyes when she woke. And it had aged her. There were lines on her face that made her look a lot older than twenty-three.

But Noah . . .

He'd gained five pounds of pure muscle. His tight black T-shirt clung to his biceps. Dark green cargo pants hung low on his hips. And his face . . .

On the drive, she'd tried to trick herself into believing he was just a friend she'd slept with one wild night. She'd made a fool of herself, losing her heart to him then.

Never again.

She'd made a promise to her broken, battered heart and she planned to keep it. She would not fall for Noah this time.

But oh, the temptation . . .

His short blond hair still looked as if he'd just run his hands through it. Stubble, the same color as his hair, covered his jaw. He'd forgotten to shave, or just didn't give a damn. But his familiar blue eyes left her ready to pass out at his feet from lack of oxygen.

He stared at her, wariness radiating from those blue depths. Five years ago, he'd smiled at her and it had touched his eyes. Not now.

"Josie?" His brow knitted as if he'd had to search his memory for her name. His grip tightened on the door. Was he debating whether to slam it in her face and pretend his mind had been playing tricks on him?

"Hi, Noah." She placed her right boot in the doorway, determined to follow him inside if he tried to shut her out.

"You're back," he said as if putting together the pieces of a puzzle. But still no hint of the warm, welcoming smile he'd worn with an easy-going grace five years ago.

"I guess you didn't get the carrier pigeon," she said, forcing a smile. *Please let him remember.* "But I need your help."

NOAH STARED AT the dark-haired beauty. Her white T-shirt hugged her curves, and her cutoff jean shorts sent him on a trip down memory lane. And those boots . . .

The memory of Josephine Fairmore had followed him to hell and back. He'd tried to escape the feel of her full lips, the taste of her mouth, her body pressed up against his . . . and he'd failed. He'd carried every detail of that night in the barn with him to basic training. Right down to her cowgirl boots. He'd dreamed about Josie in a bikini, Josie on the mechanical bull, Josie damn near *anywhere*, while hiking through the Afghan desert. He'd spent years lying in makeshift barracks wanting and wishing for a chance to talk to her while staring into her large green eyes.

And yeah, who was he kidding? His gaze would head south and he'd let himself drink in the sight of her breasts.

He closed his eyes. He'd spent two long deployments hoping for an email, a letter—something from her. He'd wanted confirmation that she was all right. But she never wrote. Not once. She'd reduced him to begging for tidbits from Dominic. Not that her brother had volunteered much more than a *She's fine. Stay the hell away from her.*

But she wasn't fine.

He opened his eyes.

"You needed help and you sent a pigeon?" He released his grip on the door and rested his forearm against it. "You could have called."

"I thought it would be better to apply for a job in person," she said, her voice low and so damn sultry that his dick was on the verge of responding.

Not going to happen.

There were a helluva lot of things beyond his control. His dad's health. His grandmother's heart failure while he was stationed in Bumblefuck, Afghanistan, fighting two enemies—and one of them should have been on his side. And the fact that the only time he felt calm, in control, and something bordering on happiness, was at the damn shooting range.

Still, he could control his own dick.

But why the hell should I?

He let his gaze drift to her chest, down her hips, and down her slim legs. He'd wanted her for five long years and here she was on his doorstep. What was stopping him from pulling her close and starting where they'd left off five years ago? He wasn't the good guy worried about her big brother's reactions or her reputation. Not anymore. Nothing he'd done in the past five years had left him feeling heroic. So why start now?

She crossed her arms in front of her chest. And while

he appreciated the way her breasts lifted, he raised his gaze to meet hers.

"I'm not hiring," he lied. Big Buck's needed a waitress or two, another bartender, and a dishwasher to keep up with the crowds pouring in from the nearby university, desperate to bump and grind to house music. But if she worked here, well hell, then he'd have another reason he shouldn't touch her. He had a rule about messing around with his female employees. It was bad business. He'd worked too hard to turn Big Buck's into something to fool around with a waitress or a bartender.

She raised an eyebrow and nodded to the Help Wanted sign he'd put up in the window. "Someone put that up without asking you?"

Shit.

"I recently filled the position," he said, searching for an excuse that didn't touch on the truth.

"I'm too late." She shook her head. "Perfect. I guess I should have gotten up the nerve to come home a few days ago."

He glanced over her shoulder and saw a red Mini parked beside his truck. It looked like a toy next to his F-250. And apart from the driver's side, every cubic inch appeared stuffed with bags.

"I thought you liked Portland. Greg from the station said you haven't been back here in a few years," he said, knowing he should close the door and end the conversation. If he let her in, if he handed her an application followed by a Big Buck's apron, he couldn't touch her. That wasn't much different from the past five years, or the ones before the going away party, but she hadn't spent the past decade or so within arm's reach.

"It didn't work out," she said.

"They don't have jobs up there for someone with a fancy degree? I bet you could do a lot better than serving drinks."

She blinked and for a second he thought she might turn around and walk away, abandoning her plea for help. "I took a break from school, lost my scholarship, and then dropped out," she said.

"What?" He stared at her. "Dominic never said—"

"My dad didn't know I'd quit school until recently. And I don't think he told Dom," she said quickly. "My brother has enough to worry about over there. Like not getting killed or . . ."

"Worse," he supplied. Like losing a limb or a fellow soldier. Yeah, Noah knew plenty of guys who'd lost both. But he'd worried about losing respect for the band of brothers serving with him because they'd flat out refused to treat the woman busting her ass alongside them with an ounce of decency . . .

Except Dominic would probably have stepped in and saved the woman before she was attacked. Josie's brother wouldn't let the situation get beyond his control and then try to pick up the pieces.

"There are worse things than dying out there," he added, trying to focus on the here and now, not the past he couldn't change.

"Yes."

He kept his gaze locked on her face as he stepped back and placed his hand on the door again. He was ready and willing to slam it closed. She could tempt and tease him, but he refused to take his eyes off her face. Hell, he knew better than to play chicken with her breasts. Right now, with the way he wanted her, he'd lose that game.

First, he needed some time to process. He wanted space to think about the fact that things hadn't worked out for her in Portland. He needed her to leave before he pulled her close, wrapped his arms around her, and offered comfort. Before he begged to know every damn detail about what had happened.

No, he needed her gone. Because he'd learned one big life lesson from his time with the marines: he wasn't a hero. He couldn't let old habits take over, pushing him to save her. He wanted Josie's hands on him, her lips pressed against him . . . not her problems dumped at his feet. And if Josie was back in the town that had insisted on labeling her wild, holding her solely accountable for losing her panties in a hay wagon ride, then something had gone horribly wrong in Portland.

"I'm sorry," he said. "I can't—"

"I need a job, Noah." She wasn't begging, merely stating a fact. But desperation and determination clung to her words. Never a good combination.

Noah sighed. "Do you have any waitressing or bartending experience?"

"Not exactly." She forced a smile as she uncrossed her

arms and riffled through the worn black leather shoulder bag. She withdrew a manila folder and handed it to him. "But I brought my resume."

Propping the door open with his foot, he took the folder and opened it. He read over the resume and tried to figure out how a series of babysitting gigs related to serving the twenty-one-and-older crowd.

"You took a year off between working for these two families." He glanced up. "To focus on school?"

"No." Her smile faded. "I can serve drinks, Noah. I'm smart and I'm good with people. Especially strangers. And now that you've taken the "country" out of Big Buck's, I'm guessing the locals don't camp out at the bar anymore."

"Some still do." And they gave him hell for telling his dad to remove the mechanical bull. Five years and the people born and bred in this town still missed the machine that had put the "country" in Big Buck's Country Bar. Some dropped by to visit the damn thing in his dad's barn. But he'd bet no one had ridden it like Josie in the last five years.

He closed the folder and held it out to her. "Why are you so desperate to serve drinks?"

"I owe a lot of money."

Another fact. But this one led to a bucket of questions. "Your father won't help you?"

She shook her head. "This is my responsibility. He's giving me a place to stay until I get back on my feet."

The don't-mess-with-me veneer he wore like body armor cracked. If someone had hurt Josie . . . No, she wasn't his responsibility. Whatever trouble she'd found—credit card debt, bad loans—it wasn't his mess to clean up. He'd spent most of his life playing superhero, first on the football field, later for his family, and then for his fellow marines. But his last deployment—and the fallout—had made it pretty damn clear that he wasn't cut out for the role.

He couldn't help Josie Fairmore. Not this time. And he sure as hell couldn't give her a job that would keep her underfoot. He couldn't pay her to work for him and want her at the same time. It wasn't right. Maybe he was a failed hero. But he still knew right from wrong.

"Look, I need experienced waitresses and bartenders." He stepped away, ready to head back to the peace and quiet of his empty bar.

"So you haven't filled the positions?" she asked.

"I—"

"Please think about it." She removed her foot, offering him the space to slam the door. "If you can't help me, I'll have to take Daphne up on her offer to serve topless drinks at The Lost Kitten. And I'd rather keep my shirt on while I work. But one way or another, I'm going to pay back what I owe."

She turned and headed for the red Mini. He stared at her back and pictured her bending over tables. One look at her bare chest and the guys at The Lost Kitten would forget what they planned to order. He hated that mental image, but jealousy didn't dominate his senses right now.

He'd witnessed a woman sacrifice her pride and her dignity for her job. He'd fought like hell for her and he'd failed her. He couldn't change the past. What happened to Caroline was out of his hands now. Even if he wanted to help, he couldn't. She'd disappeared. If and when Caroline resurfaced, she'd be the one charged with a crime. Unauthorized absence. And his testimony? The things he'd witnessed? It wouldn't matter.

But Josie was standing in his freaking parking lot.

"I'll give you one shot," he called. She stopped and turned to face him. Her full lips formed a smile and her eyes shone with triumph.

"A trial shift," he added. "If you can keep up with a Thursday-night crowd, I'll consider giving you a job."

"Thank you," she said.

"Come back around four. And don't get too excited. Your babysitting experience won't help with a room full of college kids counting down the days until spring break."

He closed the door and turned to face the dark interior of his father's bar. Giving her a shot didn't make him a hero. But it would give him a chance to figure out why she needed the money.

About the Author

After several years on the other side of the publishing industry, **SARA JANE STONE** bid goodbye to her sales career to pursue her dream—writing romance novels. Sara Jane currently resides in New York, with her very supportive real-life hero, two lively young children, and a lazy Burmese cat. Visit her online at www.sarajanestone. com or find her on Facebook at Sara Jane Stone.

Join Sara Jane's newsletter to receive new release information, news about contests, giveaways, and more! To subscribe, visit www.sarajanestone.com and look for her newsletter entry form.

Discover great authors, exclusive offers, and more at hc.com.

Give in to your Impulses . . .
Continue reading for excerpts from
our newest Avon Impulse books.
Available now wherever ebooks are sold.

CHANGE OF HEART
by T.J. Kline

MONTANA HEARTS:
TRUE COUNTRY HERO
by Darlene Panzera

ONCE AND FOR ALL
An American Valor Novel
by Cheryl Etchison

An Excerpt from

CHANGE OF HEART
By T.J. Kline

Bad luck has plagued Leah McCarran most
of her life, until the tide turns and she lands
her new dream job as a therapist at Heart Fire
Ranch. But when her car breaks down and
she finds herself stranded, the playboy who
shows up to her rescue makes Leah wonder
if her luck just went from bad to worse.

An Excerpt from

CHANGE OF HEART

By T.J. Kline

Bad luck has plagued Leah McCarran most of her life, until the tide turns and she lands her new dream job as a therapist at Heart Fire Ranch. But when her car breaks down and she finds herself stranded, the playboy who shows up to her rescue makes Leah wonder if her luck just went from bad to worse.

Leah McCarran couldn't believe her luck as she popped the hood of her classic GTO and glanced behind her, down the deserted stretch of highway in the Northern California foothills. Steam poured from her radiator, and there wasn't a single car in sight.

She blew back a strand of her caramel-colored hair as the curl fell into her eye and caught on her mascaraed eyelashes. Even those felt like they were melting into solid clumps on her eyes. It was sweltering for mid-May, and, of course, her car decided to take a dump on the side of the highway today. She fanned herself with one hand as she looked down at the overheated engine. It probably wouldn't have been nearly this big a deal if her cell phone hadn't just taken a crap, too. To top off her miserable day, she'd spilled her iced coffee all over the damn thing getting out of the car and likely destroyed it once and for all.

This wasn't the way she'd hoped to start her new job or her new life at Heart Fire Ranch.

Walking back to the driver's side of the car, Leah had no clue what to do now. Luckily, her boss wasn't expecting her until this evening, and she'd had the foresight, knowing her penchant for bad luck, to leave early. But until some Good Samaritan decided to drive by *and* stop for her, she was S.O.L. She kicked the tire as she walked by. As if trying to deny her even that small measure of satisfaction, the sole of her worn combat boot caught in the tread, nearly making her fall over.

"Son of a—"

Leah caught herself against the side of the car, willing the tears of frustration to subside, back into the vault where they belonged. That was one thing she'd learned as a child: tears meant weakness.

And showing weakness was asking for more pain.

She bent over into the car, looking for something to mop up the sticky mess the coffee was making on the restored leather interior of her car. She reached for the denim shirt she'd been wearing over her tank top before she'd left Chowchilla this morning, before the air had turned from chilled to hell-on-earth-hot.

"Shit," she muttered. Trying to sop up coffee with denim was like trying to mop a floor with a broom: it did absolutely no good.

"Hot damn! That is the most incredible thing I've seen all day."

The crunch of tires pulling off the asphalt of the highway was a welcome sound, but the awe she heard in the husky voice was enough to send a chill down her spine. Leah threw the shirt down onto the coffee-soaked floorboard. Standing up, she spun on the heel of her boot, her fists clenching at her sides as she tried to control the instinct to punch a man in the mouth.

"Excuse me? Do you really have so little class?"

"Oh, shit! No, that's not . . ." She watched as the man unfolded himself from a late model Challenger and shut the door, jogging across the empty two-lane highway to her side. "I'm sorry, I meant the car."

Leah crossed her arms under her breasts and arched a single, disbelieving brow. "Sure, you did."

A blush flooded his dark caramel skin. "I swear I meant the car. Not that you're not . . . I mean . . . crap." He cursed again. "Let me try this again. Do you need some help?"

An Excerpt from

MONTANA HEARTS: TRUE COUNTRY HERO

By Darlene Panzera

For Jace Aldridge, the chase is half the fun. The famous rodeo rider has spent most of life chasing down steers and championship rodeo belts, but after an accident in the arena, his career is put on temporary hold. When he's offered a chance to stay at Collins Country Cabins, Jace jumps at the opportunity to spend more time with the beautiful but wary Delaney Collins.

An Excerpt from

MONTANA HEARTS:
TRUE COUNTRY HERO

by Darlene Panzera

For Jace Aldridge, the chase is half the fun. The famous rodeo rider has spent most of his life chasing down aces and championship rodeo belts, but after an accident in the arena, his career is put on temporary hold. When he's offered a chance to stay at Collins Country Cabins, Jace jumps at the opportunity to spend more time with the beautiful but weary Delaney Collins.

The cowboy winked at her. Delaney Collins lowered her camera lens and glanced around twice to make sure, but no one else behind the roping chute was looking his direction. Heat flooded her cheeks as he followed up the wink with a grin, and a multitude of wary warnings sounded off in her heart. The last thing she'd wanted was to catch the rodeo circuit star's interest. She pretended to adjust the settings, then raised the camera to her eye once again, determined to fulfill her duty and take the required photos of the handsome dark-haired devil.

Except he wouldn't stand still. He climbed off his buckskin horse, handed the reins to a nearby gatekeeper, gave a young kid in the stands a high five, and then walked straight toward her.

Delaney tightened her hold on the camera, wishing she could stay hidden behind the lens, and considered several different ways to slip away unnoticed. But she knew she couldn't avoid him forever. Not when it was her job to shadow the guy and capture the highlights from his steer-wrestling runs. Maybe he only wanted to check in to make sure she was getting the right shots?

Most cowboys like Jace Aldridge had large egos to match their championship-sized belt buckles, one reason she usually avoided these events and preferred capturing images of plants and animals. But when the lead photographer for *True Montana Magazine* called in sick before the event and they needed a fill-in, Delaney had been both honored and excited to accept the position. Perhaps after the magazine viewed her work, they'd hire her for more photo ops. Then she wouldn't have to rely solely on the profits from her share of her family's guest ranch to support herself.

She swallowed hard as the stocky, dark-haired figure, whose image continuously graced the cover of every western periodical, smiled, his eyes on her—yes, definitely her—as he drew near.

He stretched out his hand. "Jace Aldridge."

She stared at his chapped knuckles. Beside her, Sammy Jo gave her arm a discreet nudge, urging her to accept his handshake. After all, it would be impolite to refuse. Even if, in addition to riding rodeo, he was a hunter, an adversary of the animals she and her wildlife rescue group regularly sought to save.

Lifting her gaze to meet his, she replied, "Delaney Collins."

"Nice to meet you," Jace said, his rich, baritone voice smooth and . . . dangerously distracting. His hand gave hers a warm squeeze, and although he glanced toward Sammy Jo to include her in his greeting, it was clear who held his real interest. "Are you with the press?"

Delaney glanced down at the Canon EOS 7D with its high-definition 20.2 megapixel zoom lens hanging down from the strap around her neck. "Yes. I'm taking photos for *True Montana*."

The edges of his mouth curved into another smile. "I haven't seen you around before."

"I—I'm not around much, but Sammy Jo here," she said, motioning toward her friend to divert his attention, "used to race barrels. You must know her. Sammy Jo Macpherson?"

Jace gave her friend a brief nod. "I believe we've met."

"Del's a great photographer," Sammy Jo said, bouncing the attention back to her.

Jace grinned. "I bet."

"It's the lens," Delaney said, averting her gaze, and Sammy Jo shot her a disgruntled look as if to say, *Smarten up, this guy's in to you. Don't blow it!*

Except she had no desire to get involved in a relationship right now. And definitely not one *with a hunter*. She needed to focus on her two-and-a-half-year-old daughter, Meghan, and help her family's guest ranch bring in enough money to support them.

An Excerpt from

ONCE AND FOR ALL
An American Valor Novel
By Cheryl Etchison

Staff Sergeant Danny MacGregor has always said
military and matrimony don't mix, but if there's
one person he would break all his rules for, it's
Bree—his first friend, first love, first everything.

Bree Dunbar has battled cancer, twice. What
she wants most is a fresh start. By some
miracle her wish is granted, but it comes
with one major string attached—the man
who broke her heart ten years before.

The rules for this marriage of convenience are
simple: when she's ready to stand on her own two
feet, she'll walk away and he'll let her go. Only,
things don't always go according to plan . . .

An Excerpt from

ONCE AND FOR ALL

An American Valor Novel

By Cheryl Etchison

Staff Sergeant Danny MacGregor has always said military and matrimony don't mix, but if there's one person he would break all his rules for, it's Bree—his best friend, first love, first everything.

Bree Dunbar has battled cancer twice. What she wants most is a fresh start. By some miracle her wish is granted, but it comes with one major string attached—the man who broke her heart ten years before.

The rules for this marriage of convenience are simple: when she's ready to stand on her own two feet, she'll walk away and he'll let her go. Only things don't always go according to plan...

She pulled into the garage of her parents' home and stared in the rearview mirror at the house across the street where Danny used to live. The same one where he was now staying. She had no idea how much longer he'd be in town, but odds weren't in her favor he would just leave her be. She'd thrown down the gauntlet and Daniel Patrick MacGregor had never been one to back down from a challenge.

Hitting the garage remote, the house slowly disappeared from view as the door lowered to the ground. Bree headed inside, her mother greeting her at the back door as she opened it.

"Can I help you carry some things in?" she asked while drying her hands on a dish towel.

"Nothing to bring in."

Bree scooted past her mother, not yet ready to rehash the morning's events.

"I thought you were going to the store?"

"I'll go back later."

She grabbed the ibuprofen from the cabinet by the sink, the dull ache behind her eyes now reaching epic proportions.

After swallowing two small tablets with a single drink of water, she headed for her bedroom.

"Is everything okay, sweetheart? You look flushed."

"Fine," she said, ducking out of her mother's reach. Twenty-eight years old and her mother still wanted to check her temperature with the back of her hand.

"Are you sure? You're not running a fever, are you? Your immune system still isn't where it needs to be. You need to be careful—"

"I'm fine, Mom. I swear. Just going to lie down for a bit."

Bree darted upstairs, escaping to the relative peace and quiet of her bedroom. She closed the door behind her, sighing in relief to see her mother wasn't hot on her heels.

She loved her dearly and wouldn't have survived chemo treatments without her, but sometimes her mother's care and concern was too much. Suffocating. And despite her best intentions, she was always reminding Bree that she'd been very sick, when all Bree wanted to do was put it behind her.

For now, she'd settle for crawling into bed and trying to forget the morning ever happened. As she closed the blinds, a familiar old truck pulled into the driveway across the street. The door flung open, and booted feet hit the concrete. Instinctively she jumped back from the window, not wanting Danny to think she'd been standing there, watching, waiting all this time for him to return home.

Bree held her breath and with the tips of her fingers lifted a single wooden slat so she could peek out. The old truck's passenger door sat open wide, but there was no sign of either brother. The screen door swung open and Danny bounded down the porch steps, reaching the truck in four long strides.

He grabbed the last few grocery bags from the floorboard and shoved the door closed with his elbow. On his way back into the house he suddenly stopped and turned to look across the street. At her house. At her bedroom window.

Despite peering through a tiny gap no wider than an inch, she knew he could somehow see her. She could feel his gaze locked on hers. But he didn't drop the grocery bags on the front porch or storm across the street toward her. Instead, he just stood there. His expression completely unreadable.

Surely he wouldn't march across the street and start things up again right now? He wouldn't dare.

Oh, but he would.

Maybe he expected her to do something. Wave. Stick out her tongue. Flip him the bird. Instead, like a deer caught in a hunter's sight, she stood frozen, unable to will herself away from the window. Then he did the very last thing she expected him to do.

He smiled.

A smile so wide, so bright, she hadn't seen the likes of one in over a decade. Although she didn't want to admit it, she'd missed that smile desperately and her heart squeezed painfully in her chest. Finally, Danny looked away, breaking eye contact, releasing her from his spell. As he turned to go inside, he shook his head, apparently unable to believe it himself.

For a long time after he went inside, Bree stood there looking out the window. And the more she replayed it in her mind, the more she began to wonder if she'd imagined the entire thing.

Only one thing was for certain—things between them were far from over.